Pitching Tents

Gail Mount

Texas Review Press

Huntsville, Texas

FIRST EDITION, 2005

Requests for permission to reproduce material from this work should be sent to:

Permissions
Texas Review Press
English Department
Sam Houston State University
Huntsville, TX 77341-2146

Cover graphics and design by E.C. Mount

Photograph of Gail Mount by Jamie Mount

Library of Congress Cataloging-in-Publication Data

Mount, Gail.
  Pitching tents / Gail Mount.-- 1st ed.
     p. cm.
  ISBN 1-881515-76-1 (alk. paper)
  1. Fort Worth (Tex.)--Fiction. 2. Fort Worth Region (Tex.)--Fiction. I. Title.
  PS3613.O856P58 2005
  813'.6--dc22

                                                            2005013687

Fred Maeder (signature)

Pitching Tents

For Dr. Hammonds –
Supreme reggie
Excellent Podiatrist
Interesting man –
a privilege to know you;
& thank you
my feet thank you.

Fred Maeder (signature)
4/10/07

Pitching Tents

To Elizabeth

Table of Contents

Pitching Tents

Part One

Storms and Ashes

1

Until I saw Vida and fell in love with her for a second time, I was dreaming of being on the loose again. The way my mother chewed the grilled cheese sandwich was about to drive me up the wall. I didn't mind so much she had to have food forbidden at the home, but looking after her and the hot May day made me want to strike out across the country.

I took a sip of ice tea and amused myself with the thought of laying down one more sear across Sage County. I took a deep breath, another sip and looked at the pictures on the walls.

I'd painted the field of sunflowers and the still life of an apple, a pistol, and a gourd dipper. I had not painted the picture of the old fellow with the know-it-all look seated at the table. You could hear his wife out in the kitchen ragging him for being so damn fool smart. Nor had I painted Jesus among the children. I'd painted more than one Jesus on black velvet, but not this one.

My mother smiled, then coughed and choked and spit up. She wiped her mouth and took a big sip of Coke. She smiled again. She was good at being mean funny.

I looked at the picture of the blood-red eighteen-wheeler coming full blast out of the night rain and wished I'd painted it.

I sighed as I felt the soft hand on my shoulder. Isabel gave me a gentle squeeze and said, "What do you have for me today, Wayman?"

I gave her the watercolor of the Hereford bull standing in a field of bluebonnets, a better picture than I'd hoped for. The orange and blue were vibrant against each other.

"I like bulls," she said playfully. Isabel was a sexy pigeon of a woman, a former Mormon who called her diner The Cafe Moroney, deliberately misspelling the angel's name to annoy her ex and her missionary son.

"I'm a little late," I said. When my tickets began to pile up and I was short of money, I'd pay with a drawing or a watercolor, if not an oil.

"I like his eyes," she said. She whispered in my ear, "Is there a chance you know a man with comparable orbs you could send me?" She started to laugh but was drowned out by a voice saying grace loud enough to shame us all.

"In Jesus' name. Amen."

I looked at the ceiling and said louder than I intended, "Poor Jesus. Poor, poor man."

I was sorry as soon as the words left my mouth. My mother cut her eyes at me like a snake. The diners grinned like there's going to be trouble for sure.

I hoped nothing major, at least not from the crusher truck drivers (who had bellies like cement trucks), and not from the farmers with baked noses and red necks, and certainly not from the young men with sharp eyes and thick necks who fought Saturday nights at the Free Cemetery or at Burro's Squared Circle or at the lake or in downtown Causeway, or anywhere they could find a good fight.

One of them whispered, "What's your trouble, old man?" and grinned.

I took it as a question I didn't have to answer.

The people of Burro had never known quite what to make of me. To some, I was a sixty-five-year-old nut; to others, I was the oldest hippie left in creation. I was neither. I was an itinerant painter on the frontier of commerce, a peddler of whatever kind of art you needed.

Still to others, I was a shade mad. Which was all right because artists were supposed to be touched in the head. After all, why would a sane man have had six wives and spent most of his life roaming the countryside in a milk truck converted into a studio?

A few of the townspeople considered me respectable since I looked out after my mother, albeit in a half-assed sort of way.

The diners went back to their fried ham, their chicken fried steaks, navy beans loaded with ham hocks, greens covered with bacon grease, creamed corn, mashed potatoes with gravy, buttered rolls, heaping bowls of cherry cobbler and banana pudding.

"Your mouth get the better of you again, Ezekiel?"

The man knew better than to call me Ezekiel. I had whipped him more than once when we were boys for calling me by my middle name.

"You wouldn't mind repeating what you said, would you? You're not ashamed, are you?" He had that same, loud-mouthed, bullying way he'd always had.

"No, I'm not ashamed. But I am sick and tired of all your Jesusing."

"That kind of talk offends my faith."

"Your kind of faith offends a lot of people. God help us if you're the religious conscience of Burro." I got a snicker here and there.

Isabel looked skittish. I gave her a wink and stood up and stretched. I wasn't the biggest man around, but I was tall and blessed with strong bones and good muscles. Life had taken a toll or two, but I was stronger than many men. My tormentor ought to know that.

"Here, everybody." Isabel was eager to make peace. "Look at Wayman's picture. Isn't it pretty?" She smiled and held it up so all could see.

"What's to see, a broken-down old bull stumbling around in a bunch of weeds? Anybody can do 'at."

That did it. My red hair was turning gray, but not my temper. My temper said now was as good a time as any to whip his butt once more. I was just about to make the offer when Vida Singer said, "You should take up art, Henry. You might make some money and improve your disposition."

The diners snickered, and I laughed out loud.

Vida Singer said, "You watch yourself, Ezekiel." She got a good laugh, which was all right.

Vida Singer could call me anything she wanted. She was tall and rangy and lived on another plateau. How could a man not love her?

"It's time you two shook hands. You all have been at each other since you were in my class. Time to quit acting like tough little nuts. Truth be known, you all weren't so tough." She sized us both up.

"Yes, ma'am, Miss Singer." The fire went out of Henry.

I'd never liked Henry and wasn't about to start now, but I offered my hand. He refused it and tried to bump me with his belly as he left. I stepped back and he nearly fell. He did a good sulk, then stomped on out.

"I did my best, Vida." I caught myself and apologized. "Sorry, Miss Singer."

"That's all right, Wayman. I should be Vida to you by now."

"I didn't know you were back."

"Well, here I am. I've been back a month or so. I don't remember exactly how long." She took off her wide-brimmed hat and smoothed her hair in a way that took my breath. "You look good, Wayman Ezekiel Scott. We should get together sometime."

I felt like a boy.

She started to leave. My mother had been watching her like a starving hawk.

"You remember my mother," I said.

"Your daughter?" Vida knew better than that.

"No, I'm his wife."

"His mother-wife. How very interesting."

"Whoa! Not my wife. No more wives for me."

"Then who am I?"

"My mother," I said. "My mother."

"And who am I?" Vida teased, leaning against me, rubbing my back.

"My first love," I said. "I fell in love with you when I was six and you showed me I could draw."

"Oh, yes," Vida said in a falling way. "Come see me sometime soon, Wayman. Please."

"Come see you? He won't even come see his own mother."

"That's a fine picture, Wayman. Bye all, I have errands to run."

The men stood as she passed.

"I want to go for a ride. I want some frozen yogurt," my mother said.

"Sure," I said, in love with Vida Singer for the second time, but in a different way this time. How peculiar and how quickly it had happened. I didn't even know where she lived, but I'd find her. First, I had to get my mother some frozen yogurt.

The closest place was in Sapient, the county seat of Sage County, a nice drive and an excuse for staying away from the home a little longer.

2

We came over a slight rise. A small valley lay stretched out in a blue haze, which clung to the grass and the grazing Holsteins.

"How pretty," my mother said.

While we ate our frozen yogurt, I admired the courthouse with its turrets. The men who built it had to have thought they were building something beautiful for the ages.

"Is it true?" my mother asked, "The reason you married so many times is you couldn't find anyone as perfect as me?"

I'd told her that once in a moment of weakness, hoping to shut her up. It didn't work.

The woman was doing her best to hold on. She was stooped and growing thinner by the day. She'd once been a voluptuous, erect, full-breasted girl brimming with life. I wondered how many lovers she'd had. None of my business, but I wondered anyway.

"You don't have to answer. I already know the answer. I'll outlive Miss Prissy Bitch Vida Singer." Her eyes sparkled. "You'll see."

Whatever Vida was, she wasn't Miss Prissy. The Bitch part, maybe.

"You have yogurt on your cheek," I said and wiped it off.

"I've outlived most everybody else. Your father, his parents, his uncles, his two brothers and sisters, the bitches." She rarely missed an opportunity to list those who had gone on before her. She took a breath. "My parents, my three brothers, my three sisters, all of my cousins and most of my friends." She gave me a hard and steady look. "And two of your children." She did not call them her grandchildren.

"True," I said.

"I may outlive you," she said cheerily.

Which was all right with me. We drove back in silence.

She frowned when we turned in the drive to the home. She claimed she hated the home, even though it had saved her life. It gave her a good diet, routine, attention, and a community to rag.

She smiled when she saw her preacher waiting on the sidewalk. Some preacher. The son of a bitch thought what money she had was his for the taking.

She cooed at him then fixed me with one of her hard looks.

"I can be determined and mean when I want." She let that sink in. "I'll see Miss Prissy Bitch in her grave and you too if you're not careful." Like she was about to ask God to put a contract out on us.

"Is something wrong, Miz Scott?" Unctuous wouldn't look at me. "May I help?"

She squeezed the man's arm and took strength. "She's too old for you anyway."

I surprised her with a kiss. "See you soon." I smiled. "Reverend."

"Mr. Scott, if you ever feel the need, just call or drop by. I'm always available."

I bit my tongue and managed a be-seein'-you smile and headed for the lake, where I went to work, trying to catch the sun on the changing surface. I had little luck. My mind was on Vida Singer, wondering where she'd been, where she was, what she was up to. I even had a jealous thought, How many loves had she known, was she in love now? If she was, so what? What about me?

What if we were a little long in the tooth? What if she was fifteen years older'n me? We weren't dead. The two of us should be in love.

The lake was drying up fast. It needed a good rain. Vida Singer was new rain in my life. No reason I couldn't break any drought in hers.

I shook my head. I had to be in love to have a thought like that. I felt better and went on home.

3

My place was a stone house over a hundred years old, built on a knoll. It was a good and comfortable base with high ceilings, excellent cross ventilation and plenty of good light, a place where my ancestors had fought off Apaches and Kiowas and where I tried to keep body and soul together.

I spent two days cleaning and scrubbing and vacuuming, cataloguing my paintings, tending to my paints and brushes, interrupted only by Vida Singer dashing through my mind.

Then as movie cowboys used to say, supplies began to run short. Maybe someone had signed up for art lessons at the Burro Art Gallery or even bought a picture. Money and beans on the table were good enough reasons to go to town. Plus, I might see Vida.

I saddled up and headed out. Everything was dusty and dry. It hurt to look at the creeks with their cracked beds. A lot of trees had died, but not the mesquites, their roots went deep for water. I had done more than one good picture of mesquites.

I felt sorry for the cattle. I didn't necessarily like the moody beasts, but I respected them.

When I was a boy, I watched a cow flat-foot it over a five-foot fence. And not too long ago I had been chased by a Brahma bull that jumped across a twenty-foot cattle guard to get at my skinny ass because me and my easel didn't belong where we were.

I'd stopped to paint a newborn calf basking in the trick of his birth. The momma cow was the proud mother as the other cows gathered around.

I'm not a great sentimentalist, but I'll never forget how good that calf and momma cow made me feel. Neither will I forget how good it was to roll under that bob-wire ahead of that bull.

I imagined Vida would've enjoyed the calf and his momma and laughed at my running for my life.

Then I was in downtown Burro, cruising Burro's famous Squared Circle, past the drugstore, the bank, the racket store and beauty parlor, the post office, filling station, the hardware store, JAKE'S, and the volunteer fire department. I stopped at the gallery. No one had signed up for a course, but a couple of my watercolors had sold. Not bad, not bad at all. But no sign of Vida.

I decided to drop by JAKE'S. The store was nothing more than a large dark hole in the wall, an old fashioned store that carried snuff and chewing tobacco, a variety of matches, country-fresh guinea eggs, homemade sausage, freshly slaughtered beef, venison now and then, plus sacks of potatoes and onions, flour and cornmeal and dried pinto beans, not to say good homemade bread, work clothes, memorabilia from the wars and Big Little Books.

If Jake were there, he would know where Vida was. Jake kept JAKE'S more as a pet than anything, but he liked it that people still shopped there.

He wasn't a landowner of multiple properties for nothing. He wasn't the County Judge for nothing. He wasn't a political force well beyond Sage County for nothing. He was a man hard to figure and hard to ignore, no man to fool with. He might have a sing-songy voice, a big behind and tits like a sow, but he had hard eyes, buckets of iron in him and a mean sense of humor.

I stood on the board sidewalk and hesitated. Then I let the screen door slam behind me. It took a while to get used to the light.

Vida was there, face to face with Jake himself. Lorrain and the boy, who were damn close to being his private property, stood in the background.

Vida ignored me. "I've come for what's mine."

"Jawbreaker?" Jake asked.

Vida took the candy and rolled it across the bare floor.

"I've come for my property, not to fool around."

"In a minute, Miss Vida. —So nice to see you, Wayman. I saw some of your watercolors at Fort Seneca. Not bad, not bad at all. Let me shake your hand."

Before I could stop him, he grabbed my hand and scratched the palm.

He laughed, "I've been asking you for some since we were in the first grade. You've always refused me, you prig." He gave me back my hand with a wink.

"I said I've come for what's mine." Vida looked tough, but Jake smiled graciously and motioned for the boy to come to him. He draped a possessive arm over the kid while giving me a teasing look. The boy was scarcely fourteen and rail thin, a sunken-chested youth with strange eyes. I felt like shaking him hard and telling him there were better pleasures than being Jake's punk. Jake whispered in his ear and the boy began to sweep up.

"I'm waiting, Jake," Vida said.

"Don't keep her waiting," I said, ready for a battle.

"In a minute, you two. Don't be so impatient."

Lorrain stepped out of the shadows. "You need me, Mister Jake?"

"Not at the moment, Lorrain, but stick around."

Lorrain was a saucy woman loyal to Jake. She was a woman with a warm smile, fire in her eyes, huge breasts and a roll of fat around her middle. A childhood bout with scarlet fever had left her a little off.

People swore Jake had acquired her off a Gypsy circus forty years ago. No matter the weather, she wrapped herself in a long shawl and a flowered dress, going barefoot and letting her wild hair flow. Her feet looked immune to heat and ice and nails alike.

"You want me to get a lawyer?"

"No need for that." Jake clucked like a mother hen.

Lorrain gave me a warm smile. I'd come up on her washing herself back in a sheltered cove at the lake. I stood as quiet as I could, hoping she wouldn't see me, wondering how she got there. She looked as native to the spot as one of the trees. She kept on about her business and didn't shy away when she saw me.

I did my best to catch her elusive face, the color of her olive breasts with nipples like dates. Her thighs were like smoothed, oiled logs. Her belly was the color of dark sand. Her pubes were shaved clean.

She finished bathing and held her arms out to me. I put a twenty on the ground and left, hoping not to offend. The resulting picture was one of the best things I ever did. I should have given her more.

Jake smiled his sly grin at us, but went on talking to Vida.

"Why on earth do you need a lawyer?"

"To get what's mine, to claim my rightful property."

"To get what's mine, to claim my rightful property," Jake mimicked.

"Yes. Violet's dead and she left the property to me," Vida said as calm as could be.

"So she is and so she did. I didn't realize you and your sister were so close." Jake sucked on his lower lip.

"The place is mine," Vida said.

"No, it's mine." There was no sucking on his lower lip or mimicking this time. "I had to take it over for back taxes. Better me than some stranger. God knows we tried to find you, but we couldn't." He looked pleased.

"I could go to Sheriff Gilchrist," she said.

"So you could." Jake was enjoying himself so much I was about ready to take an immediate physical interest.

"The house is going to rot and ruin," Vida said.

"A town lot is never completely worthless."

"My mind's made up. I'm moving in."

"Is that so?"

"Yes, that's so." Vida couldn't help herself, she laughed. Then she said so Jake would not mistake her meaning, "I'm moving in."

"And if you try to stop her, we'll go to the authorities," I said, every bit the schoolboy.

"To whom?" Jake laughed and raised an eyebrow.

"To the authorities," I said. Vida looked at me like *Please, let me handle this.* Jake giggled.

"What authorities, Wayman? I'm the authorities."

"Guess we'll see you in court or in Hell then," Vida said.

"Fine. I have courts for breakfast and no fear of Hell."

Jake the big cat licked his lips and said, "Tell you what, Miss Singer. We'll work something out. The place needs someone, so you go ahead and move in. I'll send Lorrain over."

"Thanks, Jake," Vida said and shook his hand.

"Nice to have you back, Miss Vida, even though things won't be as peaceful with you around." The man smiled and sucked at a tooth. "We haven't always been on the same side, but it was never personal on my part. I've always respected you. I hope you know that."

"Forgiveness doesn't come easy, Jake."

"I know," he said.

"Coming, Mister Scott?" Vida said as she went outside.

"Yes, ma'am."

"Hold it just a minute, Wayman." Jake grabbed me and pinched me on the butt. "I've always admired your rear."

I turned to the boy. "You ever decide to knock the Judge in the head and tell God he died, let me know. I'll be a witness."

Jake laughed.

"My love for you has never waned, not even when you ran away and did all those ugly things."

"While you stayed here and did all your ugly things."

"Well, no matter. I forgive you anyway." He had a sweet, embarrassed smile on his face. "My feelings for you will never change."

"I appreciate the consideration," I said.

Vida poked her head back in. "You don't hurry, Wayman Ezekiel, I'll send my Pennsylvania Dutch Men in after you."

"I'm coming."

"I hope you and Miss Vida and her Pennsylvania Dutch Men are all happy together." Jake laughed. "My time's coming."

4

Just as the inside of JAKE's had been dungeon dark, outside was blinding bright.

"What made him change his mind so easily, you think?"

"Maybe he knew he was overmatched." Vida grinned. She, too, was a cat.

"Maybe so."

"Or he could be in some kind of pain."

"Not the Jake I know," I said.

We had no sooner stepped off the walk when it seemed like every car and pickup in North Texas was coming at us. A bunch of turkey-necked men and women come to big Burro for the first time. To make matters worse, every kid on a bike decided to see how close they could come to us. But they didn't bother me as much as the gray heads who could barely see over their dashboards. One wrong turn, one tricky bump, and it'd be all she wrote.

As if the traffic wasn't enough, dust devils attacked. Everything swirled, from papers and wrappers to Vida's filmy peach dress. Her floppy hat took off like a flying saucer. I was lucky enough to run it down and catch it on the fly.

"Thank you, Wayman. I see the Circle hasn't changed much. No reason for it to I suppose, but one can always hope. Then I don't get to town very often. I've been out at Miss Betty's, caring for her and her pigs and her goddamned collies. No reason to come to town when you can live off what your have. Except if I hadn't made myself so scarce I'd've run into you sooner."

"Yes, ma'am. I'd've liked that."

"But I've been holed up at Miss Betty's working."

"Miss Vida, are you all right?"

"You think I'm crazy, Wayman?"

"No ma'am."

"When you're my age, Wayman, sometimes today is a century ago and fifty years past is only a second ago."

"I know the feeling."

"Families get all mixed up. Mothers become sisters, sisters aunts, cousins mothers, and fathers turn into runaway sons. I was a runaway daughter and yet, sometimes, I become all of them. —All six feet of me."

The wind stirred.

"I don't think I wore my underpants, Wayman." My heart skipped a beat. "Wouldn't that be something to see?"

"Yes, ma'am, it sure would." But it didn't happen.

"I can barely make out that old sign on the water tower. BURRO, TEXAS—HOME OF THE MEANEST. —You kids put that there, didn't you?"

"I think I was twelve or thirteen at the time."

"Remember COME SUNDOWN, NO NIGGERS, NO MESCANS, NO CHINKS?"

"I didn't paint those. I don't know what happened to 'em. They may be in the Burro museum."

"*Temps fugit*, Wayman, even if you aren't having fun." She smiled. "It was like old times. The sun in my eyes and those dust devils under my dress. I was here and there, it was all happening. Political rallies, Miss Betty's troubles and my being run off all those times. Bonnie and Clyde holed up in a cave near Paradise for a while. Pretty Boy Floyd came through and robbed the bank and kissed me. Old Man Brock shot Billy Wilson for messing around with his daughter, only it wasn't his daughter Billy was messing around with. Cars came. —I almost forgot. They built an elevated ring in the center of the Circle and you fought for some boxing championship and won. Everybody thought you were going to be champion of the world. You were so pretty. I wanted to bed you then and there after the fight."

My heart skipped another beat.

"Then you appeared with my hat and the past was gone."

"Yes, ma'am," I said.

"I need a favor," she said. "I hitch-hiked in. I need a ride."

"Sure, happy to oblige. Where to?"

"Miss Betty's. There's a surprise."

"A surprise?"

"That's what I said."

I could see being in love with Vida Singer wasn't going to be all easy. But it couldn't be all bad. She'd wanted to make love with me, even if it was a long time past.

5

As soon as we got in the truck, Vida said, "Shit!" good and hard.

"Beg pardon?"

"I said *Shit*! Don't you understand English?"

"Most of the time. What's the matter?"

"I forgot to tell Jake Miss Betty's dead."

"Mad Betty dead? I don't believe it."

"She's dead all right. I know dead when I see dead." Vida cut her eyes at me. "It's Miss Betty, not Mad Betty."

"Yes, ma'am. Sorry." But whether Miss Betty, Mad Betty or Mad Betty Bran, I didn't believe Vida. I couldn't picture Miss Mad Betty Bran dead. No way the old fury, the scourge of the county could be dead. She had to be a hundred, maybe a hundred and ten or so, but I couldn't see her dead. Maybe all she'd had was a mild stroke.

"Let's go see," I said.

Miss Betty's place was off a state highway, down a ranch road, a graveled road, a rutted dirt road, past mesquites and scrub oaks, past a pecan orchard, past blackberry bushes, poison oak and poison ivy and all sorts of tangled vines and brambles, ending in a clearing carved out of the forest.

On the way, we crossed a cattle guard and drove past a field where a bull was covering a cow.

I became so engrossed in the act, I nearly ran over a piglet. The squeals reminded me of my first pig cutting.

Then we were there. A bob-wire fence with a gate protected the place. When I got out to open the gate, a White Leghorn rooster ran at me, then went back to scratching in the brown grass. Squirrels stood and watched. I wondered where the pigs and collies were.

Horseshoes were scattered about. I hadn't pitched horseshoes since God knows when.

Rusted parts of a wagon and a tractor looked like fossils. The house didn't look like it could stand a strong breeze.

"We were fixing it up and doing all right," Vida said.

A black pot out back for making lye soap was something out of the middle ages. The barn and the privy were in better repair than the house.

"You all use the privy?"

"No, it was our joke."

"All this should be preserved," I said.

"Betty said piss on the past and I agree with her."

"What about your Pennsylvania Dutch Men?"

"A good point, but piss on them too."

It doesn't mean much today to say you're shocked and surprised, but Vida shocked and surprised me.

I just looked at her. Then I couldn't help it. I laughed.

"What's so funny?" She tilted her face back like a ten-year-old challenging her father.

"Nothing, just the thought of pissing on the past."

"Pretty funny, all right. Be careful you don't get pissed on."

"Yes, ma'am. Where's Miss Betty?"

"In the house. You can't miss her."

I hadn't seen the woman in years. What could she possibly look like? Miss Betty had come to believe bran and mash were the elixirs of life. For years she ate little else to the point her mouth became caked and crusted with bran and mash. People called her Mad Betty Bran, or Mad Betty Mash.

The woman was as short as Vida was tall. As she grew older she complained of being cold and wore enough clothes for three, whether winter or summer. She became defensive about her property and was said to walk her property lines often, and buck naked, whether in the light of a full moon or at high noon, rain or shine.

When she was no longer allowed to practice officially, her eyes became wild and wide, her hair stood on end. She looked like nature's wrath and would go into Burro to startle strangers and scare children.

"Okay," I said. "Let's go in." I had no idea what to expect. As far as I knew, she could be sitting in her favorite rocker cradling her shotgun. At one time she had been a great shot.

"Yes, let's. Miss Betty, we have company." Vida took my arm. Her eyes sparkled.

6

Mad Betty didn't answer. She wasn't in the parlor or the sewing room, the bathroom or her bed. She wasn't in her rocker with her shotgun. She was stretched out on the kitchen table with a smile on her face, eyes wide open, dead and naked. Naked naked. A funny, hard naked. Bare. Splotched and ruddy. Cold. No modesty, not even an attempt. Cold, clutching a letter across her belly.

"You thought I was crazy," Vida said.

"She's dead all right."

"Like to join me in some homemade wine? There're gallons under the sink. Gallons."

Tempting. At one time I'd loved good homemade wine, but I hadn't had a drink since my last wife left me ten years ago. A look at Mad Betty said now was a good time to start again. Then I had the feeling I was going to need what few wits I had before the day was over.

"I think I'll pass."

"I think I won't." She filled a fruit jar with ice tea for me and a fruit jar with wine for her. We toasted Miss Betty.

I'd seen a few corpses other than at funerals. Dead people out in the street, in beer joints, on the battlefield, but not one like Miss Betty with her crusted smile. She looked like she'd died of hydrophobia. Her hair radiated like frozen bolts of lightning.

"I was supposed to get Jake out here so he could see her like this, but I was so caught up in my private troubles, I forgot."

"You all planned this?"

"Betty didn't kill herself, if that's what you mean. But Betty knew she was dying. She thought a good way to pay Jake back for his meanness would be for him to see her in her natural glory." She blew her nose. "I was supposed to bring him out here. I let my friend down."

"All is not lost," I said, trying to think of another way to get him out here.

She blew her nose again and drained her jar. "I think I'll take a picture or two."

She went to look for her camera. I looked at Miss Betty. It took more than pluck to crawl up on that table to die.

I looked at her again and wished she'd get up and go in another room. —If she couldn't, I could.

The place was filled with books, pictures, carvings, maps; volumes of typed and handwritten pages, some yellowing and crumbling, but most in a readable, intelligent, graceful script. Boxes were packed with cryptic notes, ciphers and codes. I wondered how much wisdom and foolishness was packed into those volumes. I wondered if the library at Alexandria had been like this before the fire.

Then I saw the two computer monitors staring at me like alien predators. Miss Betty and Vida weren't lost in the past. They were current as Hell.

I backed away and almost stumbled over a stack of shoeboxes. So the old girls loved shoes.

I wound my way out to the kitchen where Vida was clicking away like a photographer at a wedding.

I couldn't help myself. The place had overwhelmed me. "My God, Vida, this is a holy place."

"Don't prattle, Wayman. Take Miss Betty outside. I want some pictures outside. And after I'm finished, I'm going to send Jake one a week to remind him what a bastard he was and is."

Miss Betty wasn't the easiest thing to handle, but I got us outside without falling. I laid the firm Miss Betty on the cellar door and Vida clicked away.

"It's not right, her naked and us not." Vida downed more wine and shucked her clothes in the blink of an eye. She was a shock.

"Well?" she said like the schoolteacher she was.

I didn't exactly jump up and down at the thought of getting naked, but what could I do? I was about to join the two when the collies showed up, barking and wailing and whining and sniffing.

We took some pictures of the collies and Miss Betty before Vida ran them off.

We got a fine picture of me and Vida and Miss Betty; some good ones of Miss Betty alone, Vida alone, me alone, the two of us, the three of us.

We heard the grunts and snorts long before the hogs burst up on us. Vida fended them off until I could slop them. The next time someone starts talking about the delicate, fine-tuned beauty of the universe, let 'em slop a bunch of hogs.

When I finished, Vida said, "Time to read the letter."

Vida straightened herself and read without pomp:

"'Not to worry all. I, Miss Betty, Mad Betty, Mad Betty Mash, am of sound mind as this is written.

"'I, Betty Elizabeth, my actual name, Green Johnson am going to die in about five to ten minutes, not by my own hand, the hand of God or the Devil, man or beast, but by the process of wearing out. I am neither overjoyed or over-grieved by the prospect. I had fun poking my nose into things and seeing what would happen.

"'Once I could shake the ground as well as any man. I was a stirrer-upper. I was never completely out of it. My life was a good life.

"'What I leave behind, I leave to my friend, my loved one, my lover, Vida Singer, the tall bitch.

"'Burn me or bury me, but don't wash my face. Leave the grin alone.

"'It's hard to write in this position

"'It's nice to be rid of

"'Oh, piss'"

"That's it." She gave the place a long look. "I vote for a bonfire."

"You can't burn this place down," I said.

"Why not? She liked fires."

"We might burn up the whole county."

"That would be something to see. The thought gives me the grins."

"It's against the law."

"Who's to know?" She looked around. She sighed. Her wildness became a soft smile.

"Maybe you're right, Wayman. Mustn't let my feelings get the best of me." She licked her lips. "Tell you what, put Betty in the truck and let's haul ass." She slipped into her dress in the flick of an eye.

I did as ordered. "Where to?"

"Hold your horses. I'm forgetting something. Oh, my poor mind. What is it?" She folded her arms and leaned back in the seat. I reached over to hug her. She pushed me away.

"No, not now. I want that as much as you do, but later."

I liked the thought, but it scared me.

"The shoeboxes, Wayman. The shoeboxes, the computer, the fax, and the printer. Thank you, mind." She grinned. "Don't just sit there. Go fetch them. We don't have all day. Fetch them."

Dog-like I fetched the shoeboxes, the fax, the computer and the printer.

"Look," she said. The shoeboxes were filled with legal documents, deeds, a will, and lots of money. Gold and silver coins. Twenties, fifties, hundreds, even a thousand dollar bill or two. All real and good and legal tender. Mucho dinero.

"You're rich!" I no longer felt so cross.

"Not hardly, but it is something to work with, thank goodness or whatever."

"Yes. Thank goodness or whatever. Where to?"

"To the Causeway Funereal Parlor. Know any hymns?"

"A few."

We hauled out of there singing "Onward Christian Soldiers," "The Little Church In The Wildwood," and "A Mighty Fortress Is Our God!" Vida came up with a pretty good rendition of "Amazing Grace." Betty's grin looked to grow broader and broader. Vida became prettier and prettier. I thanked The Lord and whatever. I floor boarded it, wondering what Vida was going to do with Miss Betty and with all that money.

She said, "You have to take off your clothes next time."

7

Causeway was six miles from Burro, but those six might as well have been a thousand. No love had ever been lost between the two towns, not now, not in the past and not likely in the future.

Causeway, even though a small town, was five times the size of Burro. A gas producer kept a branch there. A driller stacked his rigs just outside of town. The rock crusher had a truck terminal in town.

Not all that much to shout about, but that didn't keep the citizens of Causeway from being puffed up. Causeway, after all, had a daily newspaper, a municipal building, a park, a hospital, my mother's rest home, a public library, and other amenities such as four cafes, a drive-in, a motel-hotel and the funeral home. Even Burro's weekly was printed in Causeway.

Some of my stuff hung in various buildings and homes around there, but I never felt at ease in Causeway. When I was a footloose kid, I was the stranger in town, the lone gunfighter looking for trouble. As I got older, when it came to Causeway, I still had the knack.

I backed my truck into the unloading zone between the fancy white ambulance and the pitch-black hearse at the Causeway Funereal Parlor. I looked at the grinning Vida and smelled trouble. I hoped I was wrong.

Buster Two Sticks, the forty-year-old son of the owner of The Causeway Funereal Parlor, and Buster Three Sticks, his nineteen-year-old son, headed our way. The boy was stamped with his poppa's bulldog face, ruddy complexion and beer belly; plus the same mixture of piety and *lookie here more business* smile. When they recognized me, their faces flashed from the welcome of sweet sorrow to near anger. King Buster, the patriarch, and I weren't exactly friends, but he would have their hides if they chased any business away, even mine. It was fun to see their smiles turn warm again.

"I'm Vida Singer and I've come to see Mister King Buster about a delicate matter," she said disarmingly, touching the tip of a lace handkerchief to her eyes.

The Busters were supreme bastards. They'd smile and pick your pockets, all the time making you feel guilty for not doing more for your loved one, even if you didn't love the loved one. They smiled until I was ready to bury Mad Betty out on the prairie.

"Certainly, Miss Vida." Two Sticks oozed like a tar pit.

My adrenaline flowed. "If it's a fight you boys want, I'll be happy to oblige."

"What's eatin' you?" Three Sticks said. He didn't know it, but he was easy.

"Shame, Wayman, shame."

"Come on, folks, let's go see Daddy." Two Sticks was more rational.

Vida took me by the arm like she was going to break it if I didn't behave.

King Buster sure had changed. From a tall, rawboned, strong kid into a man of means, a baron with a head like a jaded old bull, topped by a mass of wavy white hair. He was red faced and greedy, given to quick, passing sympathy. He was a mountain of four hundred pounds of slosh. I hated to think what would happen if he sprung a leak. We'd drown.

"Welcome back, Miss Vida. How nice." The man was a master of slick graciousness. He stretched his arms out and made an effort to rise from his leather throne. His bulk rippled upwards, but his butt never left the chair.

He smiled. "Exercise exhausts me."

Damned if Vida didn't bend and kiss him.

"Wayman, Wayman, Wayman, my wayward Wayman," the son of a bitch, "I bought one of your watercolors the other day. Lake House. Very nice. Not many have your touch. Serene, peaceful, quiet. Unlike the colorist."

"Much obliged."

"Good to see you looking so well, Miss Vida," he said. He gestured at his walls. "I'm sure you know that French writer who lined his room with cork. Mine is lined with leather."

"Interesting," she said, "but hot."

"It is hot," he said, "even with the air conditioning. Maybe these fans will help." He winked.

I had designed those fans years ago and had never been paid. They were good, tough, reed fans decorated with the hint of a large home in the woods and dignified lettering, CAUSEWAY FUNEREAL PARLOR. King Buster figured FUNEREAL instead of FUNERAL would have a distinctive, popular appeal. He was right.

"Excuse me," Vida said. "I'm so thirsty I'm about to spit cotton."

"Bring us some lemonade, grandson." The old man's every move, his every breath was full of suspense like it might be his last.

"What brings you back, Miss Singer? It's been a while."

"I thought it might be interesting to see if things had changed."

"Have they?" Buster Uno.

"In some ways," she said softly.

The kid returned and King Buster pulled a fancy bottle of gin out of his desk.

"Sweetener, anyone?"

"For a dry county, there seems to be an overflowing supply of hooch," Vida said lyrically.

Everyone agreed with a smile and took a sip, except me and Three Sticks. I stuck to the lemonade. He took both and drained his glass in one gulp.

"I see you're still on the wagon, Ezekiel. Commendable."

"I get the feeling I could fall off anytime." I hoped not then and there. I had the feeling I was going to need all the sobriety I could muster.

"You know, Ezekiel, you won our first fight fair and square, but not the second. I had you whipped six ways from Sunday when you kicked me in the family jewels. You nearly killed me. I wasn't too happy about that. But I'm not a man to carry a grudge that long."

King Buster was right. The first fight was a fair one. I broke his nose and knocked a few teeth loose. I blacked his eyes and cut his mouth. I slapped a few knots on his head, fair and square. The rematch was different. He knocked me down and kicked me in the ribs. He was about to beat the hell out of me, the pride of Burro. I kicked him in the balls as hard as I could. He fell like a sheared Samson.

"Can you remember what we were fighting about? I don't. Wasn't pussy, was it Zeke? —Beg pardon, Miss Vida."

"Perfectly all right, King. Pussy's a worthy cause." She suddenly adopted a comical Southern manner.

"It was a matter of pride and honor between knights," I said, pissed off. "Our fights had nothing to do with pussy." The fights were still serious with me.

"My Lord. Pride and Honor. Whose?" The man imitated Vida and looked me right in the eye.

"Burro's and Causeway's," I said.

"I haven't forgotten." The man changed his manner. "Well, I've become a big man in more ways than one, and you appear to be the same, except older." Another of his sweet-mean grins. "I chose to serve my country and you went conscientious objector. A lot of people couldn't understand why a battler like you went CO."

There was no need to remind him I saw action and he didn't. He knew.

"After the war, I chose the mortuary and you chose another form of the popular arts."

"It's a funny old world," I said.

Three Sticks interrupted. "You all didn't come here just to shoot the shit." Whatever he was, he was stupid, but he wasn't shy.

"Right," Vida said, dropping her comedy. "Miss Betty Elizabeth Green Johnson died today. We're here about her last rites."

King Buster lost his breath for a scary moment.

"Sad. I know you two ladies were very close."

"That old woman with bran all over her face is dead? Well, goddamn," Three Sticks said and Vida gave him a look to freeze his blood.

"Where is she?" Two Sticks asked, afraid of the answer.

"Out in my truck."

"She might be a shade warm by now," Vida said.

"Go see!" King B. ordered.

"Isn't she pretty?" Vida said.

"Goddamn, Daddy, she's dead and she's naked."

"Go get your grandpa."

We waited. Grandpa came inching along, supported by Three Sticks on one arm and his number one illegal on the other.

The mountain lingered over Mad Betty from head to toe, from crusted smile to spare bush, from dried paps to her button of life, from her calloused feet to her electrified hair, from her splotched hands to her dead eyes.

"Somebody, please get a sheet. Son, you get Jake over here pronto."

"I don't believe it. Mad Betty Bran is dead. Mad Betty Mash is gone. Goddamn, I sure do feel sorry for the Almighty." He laughed, then turned to Vida.

"What do you have in mind, Miss Vida?"

"All in good time," she said. "Let's wait for Jake."

We went back to the office and waited. Nobody had much to say. I had lemonade, the others lemonade and gin. It wasn't too long before Jake barged in, taking charge as always. "What's going on, King?"

"Come see for yourself."

"Goddamn! It is true, no one lives forever." He caught himself. "My Aunt Betty, my favorite relative is gone. I'll miss her," he said in a breaking voice and closed his eyes as if in silent prayer. He wasn't a politician for nothing.

"Amen," Vida said.

Jake didn't look prayerful when he opened his eyes and looked at Vida.

"I mean that. No one ever meant more to me." He pecked his favorite aunt on the cheek.

"Clean her up, King. Get all that bran and mash off her face. Put some rouge and lipstick on her. Fix her hair. Put a new dress on her. She deserves it, poor thing. Poor, poor thing. Bless her heart." Sage County's leading citizen was about to weep.

King B's eyes lit up. A small smile crossed his lips. But Vida's eyes didn't twinkle; no smile crossed her lips.

"No one is going to wash her face, shampoo her hair or put a new dress on her. Miss Betty is going to have the last word."

"Now, Miss Vida, be reasonable. The least we can do is make her decent." Jake used his best sorghum molasses voice.

"I said no one is going to change her." Vida's best Fuck You look swept across her face.

"She was my aunt," Jake said, but without sweetness this time.

"She was my loved one. The best you all can do is leave her alone. The man, woman or child who so much as touches her without my permission answers to me. She left me to look after her. I intend to do just that." Vida stood between Miss Betty and them. I moved to her side. Jake and the Busters stepped back.

"How're you going to pay for it, old woman?" Two Sticks couldn't help it he was a born-and-bred asshole.

"Well, there's the five thousand dollars buried somewheres around her place. Miss Betty always said the best bank was a buried coffee can. All I have to do is dig it up. No hill for a climber."

Jake and the Busters fidgeted like little boys.

"Very well," Jake said. "You do with her what you will. That okay by you, Buster?"

"As long as I get paid."

"You boys are such good boys. You have my word you'll be paid in full. I promise."

Jake and the Busters wandered off, leaving Vida and me with Miss Betty. Vida smiled.

I stood there wondering what to do next, when luck in the form of Buster's number one illegal appeared. He was a swarthy man with dark eyes and black hair, an India ink mustache and a face that looked like desert rock.

Vida held his right arm in her best vise-like grip and began to hablay with him. The poor fellow grimaced, but he stood there and listened and nodded and whispered. Vida let go. He massaged the hell out of that sore muscle, but he didn't run off.

"We're in luck. Mi amigo tells me the crematorium fires are

ready. We'll sneak Betty Elizabeth in. Our friends won't know a thing until it's too late."

"How'd you swing that?"

"The gold-dust twins of bribery and threat. I promised money and mentioned that Sheriff Gilchrist was my dear friend. Rafael understands Sheriff Ronnie is not afraid of Jake."

Vida was pleased with her guile, but I was jealous of her affection for Ronnie.

Mad Betty was cremated without fanfare.

Vida slipped the illegal a couple of hundreds then hablayed with him some more. When he said, "Si," she gave him another couple of hundreds, mixed in with okay, gracias and de nada.

"What was that all about?"

"Patience."

"Patience? I'm near to wore out."

"Hold on, Wayman, hold on. We're almost done, only a few things left." She clapped me on the back.

8

We drove to Sapient, where Vida spent an ungodly amount of time with Sheriff Gilchrist going over some papers. Ronnie was about my age, maybe a little older, a string bean of a fellow who looked like he'd live forever. We'd known each other as boys, but had kept our distance. When he became Sheriff, the distance widened. He was a good man, but law enforcement. I gave him a wide berth most of the time.

He and Vida talked just soft enough to keep me from hearing. When they finished, Ronnie gave Vida far too long of a kiss. Vida smiled at my jealousy and said, "To Miss Betty's, James." Like the good chauffeur I was, I floorboarded it. Ronnie stuck the nose of his car up my exhaust and didn't budge.

Vida smiled. The searchers were in Miss Betty's yard, huffing and puffing and digging away. Jake and King Buster stopped when they saw us. The other two kept right on digging.

"This place looks like a prairie dog town," Vida clapped.

"You boys taking some exercise?" Ronnie asked. "It's good to see grown men at play, but King, you be careful in this heat. You don't want to overdo."

Heat was an understatement. Hardly summer and already fifteen consecutive days of a hundred or more.

Ronnie teased, "Now boys, I want a straight answer." The tease in his voice got a lot harder. "You all digging for gold or what?"

Jake got up off his knees, not embarrassed at all. He smiled and dusted his hands off on his khakis.

"I'm inspecting the premises with the thought of turning the place into a historical attraction. This house could become a first-class bed and breakfast. The barn could be a combination museum-social club. Visitors would come from far and wide. Provided you and Miss Vida don't mind." He was not going to go easy.

"I suppose then you all are taking soil samples to benefit the county." Ronnie was having a good time.

"This is my land," Jake said.

"Not according to these documents. The way they read, this here place belongs to Miss Vida Singer, free and clear and legal."

Jake grabbed at the documents.

"Easy," Ronnie said. "Easy."

Jake read and went ashen.

"Satisfied?" Ronnie asked.

Jake didn't answer.

"All right, boys, the fun's over. Trespassing's against the law. So is defacing private property."

"Are you telling us we're under arrest?" Jake's question was like a threat.

"Want me to read you your rights?" Ronnie sounded every bit as tough as Jake.

"Are we under arrest?" Jake was noticeably softer.

"Not you, Jake. And not Busters, old farts one and two, but the boy is."

"For what?" Three Sticks had a nasty way of curling his lips.

"There're five warrants out for your arrest, son."

"Bullshit!" the boy said.

"No bullshit. I've got warrants from Wallerford, Wells, Corsicana, Fort Seneca, and Causeway. The next thing you know, you'll be a real outlaw."

"What's this all about?" Two Sticks was hot.

"Tell him," Ronnie said.

"Just some speeding tickets. Nothing to get excited about."

"Nothing to get excited about?" Buster Two was as red as fresh blood.

"What the hell, I wasn't speeding. They had a hard-on for me."

"I wonder why," Vida smiled.

"Because I'm young."

"Son of a bitch!" Two Sticks sat down hard.

"Yes indeed," King Buster muttered. "Twice over."

Three Sticks took a couple of steps like he was going to bolt.

"Come on, son, don't be foolish," Ronnie said.

"You going to cuff me?"

"If I have to, but I want you to fill them holes in first. All of 'em. All of you."

There were a godawful number of holes and it was hot. Jake scooped dirt and smiled and shook his head. King Buster wheezed and crawled around like a walrus on land. He looked like he thought he was about to die and didn't like what he saw on the other side. When they finished, Three Sticks looked ready to run.

"Temptation being what it is, I'd better cuff you after all," Ronnie said.

The boy glowed at being cuffed, but his daddy didn't. King Buster offered neither blame nor praise, succor or despair. Ronnie put the boy in the back of the patrol car. Jake said they would follow them in.

"You boys find what you were looking for?" Vida asked.

"Not one coffee can, not a single dollar. A good joke, Miss Vida. A fine joke indeed." Jake broke out with a charm I'd never seen before.

"What's the matter, Jake? Ain't you got enough?"

The man looked at me with pity like I didn't understand the first thing about *enough*, that I didn't have the vaguest idea about money and possessions and power and what a strange thing that was. What a surprise, what a fool I was.

"Don't let her work you too hard, Wayman. No way in the world you can keep up with her. Right, Miss Vida?" Jake laughed like he felt really good. "See you later."

"Look forward to it," Vida said.

Ronnie asked if everything was all right in such a way my stomach winced.

Vida said everything was fine and gave him a goodbye hug, then motioned for me to come on. Jake was right. She had other work for me.

9

We took off for the Western Hi-Tone Art Gallery (And Bookstore) in Fort Seneca, about an hour's drive away.

Fort Seneca was named after the last of the fighting Kiowa chiefs. It was said by some, and I don't mean just the Chamber of Commerce, to be America's best kept secret, the one truly relaxed, laidback community in the U. S., which considering its origin was surprising.

One night Chief Seneca and his warriors were camped along the banks of the Trinity preparing to surrender the next morning, when a detachment from Sherman's or Sheridan's army attacked and wiped them out, taking no prisoners, as the saying goes. Depending on who's doing the telling, the soldiers were weary and hungry, scared shitless, or bored and wanted to see what it was like to kill someone. The spot became Fort Seneca, America's most laidback city.

I was enough of a cross-country peddler to know no one place in the good old U.S.A. was truly laidback. Not L. A. or Southern California, certainly not San Francisco, not Seattle, New England or the Carolinas, not Virginia, not the North, for God's sakes; not the Deep South or New Orleans or the Midwest; not Alaska, the baked Southwest, Hawaii, or even my beloved Texas. Some put on a show, some were a touch calmer. Some were poised and polite, but all could come to a boil without warning. A professor friend, who was only an occasional know-it-all bastard, had assured me that open violence was the order of the day, that something more than self-preservation, something more than ordinary wildness, something like destruction for destruction's sake, violent anger for the sake of violent anger, was on the loose. As if to prove the point, he was killed in a convenience store robbery. For no good reason except he was there.

Goddamn, what was happening to me? I'd been all over this country painting and selling its beauty. I'd taken a lot of nourishment from practically everyone everywhere and here I was going on like a wormy old man. Old age was making me bitter, but that couldn't be right. Vida was fifteen years older'n me and she wasn't bitter. So it had to be something other than old age.

She looked peaceful enough sitting there, riding along, watching the farms roll by. The boy in me wanted to tease her, but I didn't.

Then Fort Seneca stood before us like a redone grand dame trying her damnedest to be in step with the times, and why not? I looked for the old courthouse, but it was hidden by tall glass office buildings, new hotels, painted storefronts, an opera house, a convention center with fountains and gardens. The old girl had been given a good goose.

Her freeways were another matter. Once a marvel, moving traffic along without any fuss, they now suffered from repairs and expansion making driving difficult and dangerous. Not much *After you* cordiality; more *Get the hell out of my way* with shaken fists, wrecks, shootings, and bodies under sheets. So it was good to see billboards promising *Just A Matter Of Time Before Progress Replaces Disorder. Commerce Is On The Upswing!*

Who was I to doubt it? I was a commercial being. True, I hadn't gotten rich, so maybe I wasn't too good at it, but I hadn't starved and neither had my wives and children. I'd given it a good try. Being commercial wasn't always nice, but it had had its moments. The trick was to watch out for false prophets.

Then I saw the old courthouse sticking up like a proud old penis. I felt better.

Despite the changes, the crap and the crime, Fort Seneca was my favorite city. I liked the remaining brick streets. I liked being "Where the West begins" and didn't mind having to watch out for rattlers and stinging lizards. I remembered idling away pleasant hours watching horned toads and doodlebugs. I remembered, or imagined, the sight and smells of the stockyards alive with cattle.

I liked the self-conscious accent of the natives. I appreciated the courtesy remaining in those who still had a sense of tolerance, which had not given in to a gilded cowboy-businessman-businessman-cowboy mentality.

I told myself to ease off. I didn't have anything against progress. I hadn't led any parades against the up-to-date. What was I, some old geezer in love with a false past, a man old before his time, a man about to wither on the stalk?

"I don't know," I said aloud.

"Beg pardon?" Vida said.

"Nothing. Just talking to myself."

"I feel a lot better now." She stretched and glowed.

"That's nice," I said. The traffic was unforgiving.

"You know, Wayman, once you get a highway job, you're fixed for life. It's like pushing a rock uphill that keeps rolling back, except the pay's good and you get plenty of water. Plus you get to rest."

I didn't say anything.

She looked me up and down. "All you and I have to do is find the thread in the chaos."

I nodded. A speeding eighteen-wheeler was coming up hard and about to flatten us.

She leaned over and squeezed my thigh real hard just when it looked like we were about to become a grease spot.

I stepped on it.

"Sounds good to me," I said. I dodged a pickup with a thirty-thirty slung across the back windshield, turned off the freeway, and headed for the gallery.

10

The Western Hi-Tone Art Gallery (And Bookstore) was on the north side in an old part of town, a friendly if not provoked, respectable, near seedy area where some of the beer joints were for loving, some for fighting and some for loving and fighting.

The neighborhood had a kick to it that said, 'I was born here, I've been here all my life, don't ask me to move, I won't do it.' It was a neighborhood marked by its own musk, wary of those who wandered around looking to buy up property in order to tear it down.

Vida sniffed the air. "I like it."

Dorothy, who owned and ran the gallery and bookstore, met me with a bear hug.

"You old devil, you feel good. Too good." Her face was an outcropping of smiling rock.

She was a sixty-year-old chunk of a woman from Weslaco, an expert in all kinds of art, from what critics call the quotidian—the everyday to the rest of us—to what I call the high falutin'. She had a good eye and she knew how to sell. She didn't care if the work was sentimental or hard, pious or earthy, mirror real or scattered splotches of paint. As long as it showed her something, she would do her damnedest to sell it. We never talked about whether or not my stuff was any good. She just took it and sold it. God bless her.

"You look pretty good yourself."

She looked hard, but she was juicy and sexy. She once took on a hundred and one boys at the University in one month. I wasn't one of the hundred and one. We hadn't even made love when we painted the mural of us naked painting each other. Then I hadn't slept with many women other than six I'd married. I knew men who'd had that many in a twenty-four-hour period. I'd never had the talent. Once I'd burned and envied them. I grew not to.

Her illustrations of women making love to other women as well as a series of drawings of variously shaped and sized penises, intended to make people laugh and gasp, landed her in trouble. She even spent a night or two in jail. She was on the map.

Her stuff wasn't my style, but it was good and she'd been a good friend.

Vida coughed and said, "Wayman, are you going to stand there all day? Aren't you going to introduce me?"

"Yes, ma'am." I felt like blushing but Dorothy said, "You don't have to tell me who this is. Welcome to my life, Vida Singer." She hugged Vida like Vida was the second coming.

"I was saddened to hear about Miss Betty. She was a great woman."

The two women made some picture as they kissed surprisingly strong. The number of undergrounds in this country is amazing. With half an effort, they could turn this country upside down in no time.

"We've come to impose on you," Vida said. "We'd like to make some posters of Miss Betty." Which was news to me.

The business looked small from the outside, but its guts ran wide and deep with plenty of room for the gallery, the bookstore, storage areas, a downstairs, upstairs, a large work area with plenty of equipment, and a complete darkroom. We went right to work and it felt good. My body liked the rhythm.

Vida and Dorothy developed the pictures and I heard Dorothy say, "Nice, good, very good, fine, oh fine. You know Vida, I have some of your early movies. They're very funny."

I was too engrossed in a silk screen to wonder what they were talking about. One of the good things about being an everyday artist is you learn how to produce a lot of different kinds of work without resorting to the pure shoddy. The result may be piss poor once in a while but the effort never is. The joy is in the rhythm, like mowing a field with a scythe.

I can paint on mirrors and glass and velvet. I do lithographs, woodcuts, mixed media, blown glass, and batik with the best of them. I can cast bronze, weld steel, carve wood, sculpt in marble and stone. I'm a master at mobiles. My fiber sculptures are presentable. My watercolors, my pastels, my oils, and my acrylics are first rate. Egg white and gouache is no threat to me. I know about posters and silk screens.

We ate hot tamales and drank hot coffee to keep going. Vida was happy, Dorothy ecstatic. The poster and silk screens caught something special about Miss Betty.

"You've outdone yourself, Wayman," Dorothy said. "These are great."

She was right. I'd caught something different. The wide-eyed and naked Miss Betty looked more alive than most people ever did.

"Electric and wonderful," Vida said.

"I'm bushed."

"I can't imagine why," Dorothy said. "There's a bed upstairs. Why don't you and Vida give it a try before you both drop. Even an army has to rest."

"I'm game," Vida said.

So we went to bed. The room was nice and quiet and cool. We lay there. Our nervous energy ran out of our bodies and shook the bed. We made love in our fashion for the first time and slept like babies. When Dorothy came to wake us up, Vida said she couldn't remember being so comforted.

11

Vida was elegant in her black outfit with a wide brimmed, lemon-yellow hat. I was uncomfortable in my dark suit and starched white shirt buttoned at the collar, a garb Vida insisted on.

We had plastered Mad Betty posters all over Sage County announcing her memorial service. It was hot and hard work, but the fun part was no one could do a thing to us because Ronnie had put the word out to leave us alone. We covered King's pride and joy with the electric Mad Betty.

I was sure no one would come. But people came like the gate had been left open, another example of undergrounds. Rafael had done his work well.

Once, such a turnout of young and old, of white and black and brown and some yellow and in-between shades would've been cause for a serious ruckus, but this rainbow filled the chapel and spilled out all over the place.

The only malcontents were my mother and her preacher. They had a big time snubbing me.

The people became quiet as the organ began playing. The music was heartfelt and moving. Miss Betty's death had diminished each one of us.

Vida stood and started right in.

"Miss Betty Elizabeth Green Johnson, La Dama Loca, the Crazy Doctor, La Bruja, the Bitch Lady Witch Doctor, is dead. No longer will she tend to us, no longer will her tormentors be able to laugh at her, no longer will she be hurt.

"Betty suffered not from being too bright and generous, or from the usual meanness we all know, but from the narrow goodness of Sage County's leading citizens.

"She went to the University, where she became our first full-blown female-woman doctor; a person not to be pushed aside, or taken lightly. Betty was a woman who bowed her neck and said, long before it became empty, 'There is some shit I will not eat.' She meant it.

"She was dangerous. She taught mothers and daughters how to douche and wipe themselves. She taught men who were more ignorant than the women how to clean their foreskins and how to put a rubber on. She was very dangerous.

"She treated us all. She accepted us for the naked creatures we were, taking our farts in her face with good grace. She cured crabs, the clap, and syphilis. She set broken bones, she cut out hairballs, and more than one rotten appendix. She sewed up hernias. She fought smallpox, pneumonia, and influenza.

"Dangerous animal she was, she was at her best in delivering babies. Until the day she died, she wrote about how to be a good midwife. Many a little girl in this county has answered to the name of Betty Elizabeth, and many a boy to B. E.

"She wrote pamphlets about how to make love without conception. She fitted more than one diaphragm, tied off a tube or two, and performed vasectomies long before they became popular.

"She wrote about child bearing and child rearing. She taught some of us hillbillies how to read. She taught us, the poor, we were as good as the rich.

"The good people couldn't handle such danger. They accused her of murdering the unborn willy-nilly, of being a lesbian whore who took all colors and sexes to her arms.

"She performed abortions, not helter-skelter, but carefully out of conscience and respect.

"No matter who came to her for treatment, she took them, us, to her bosom.

"But the good people had their way. Betty was barred from practice. She was told she was lucky not to be jailed.

"But the dangerous lady didn't break. She went underground. The authorities hounded after, saying she copulated with beasts. They had her declared insane and sent away. But she came back, covered with bran and mash, sometimes walking naked whenever the mood struck.

"The well meaning couldn't stop her.

"Betty Elizabeth Green Johnson, our dangerous animal, is dead, leaving us to live on the wing. God knows why she loved us, but she did. So, here we are with our saddened love, celebrating her."

Vida finished. Everyone was joyous, except my mother and her preacher.

"Your Miss Vida is next," my mother whispered.

"Not the most Christian of services," Reverend Dan said.

Vida took a breath and looked the man over and said quietly, "Not to worry. Miss Betty was a pagan in good standing. I don't think the Trinity minds, but if they do, so be it."

"Be careful of sacrilege. You may burn forever," the man said quietly.

I'm not sure what Vida said next, but I think it was, "I don't give a fuck if I do."

Whatever she said, it was something dangerous, because Ronnie came over and said, "Best for everybody to be careful."

I didn't say a word. People came and hugged Jake, saying how sorry they were for his loss, how much they admired and loved his aunt; that he must have loved her deeply, that he must be deeply grieved. The man didn't smile or cry.

King Buster was satisfied. He got his money.

I looked forward to a long sleep, but Vida said, "Just a bit more and we're finished."

"Where to now?"

"The old Doe place. You know where it is?"

12

Of course I did. Everybody knew the old Doe place. A few years ago, Hillman Doe was constantly in the news. He was a man of fifty at the time and depending on who you talked to, a troublemaker, a murderer, a revolutionary, a voluptuary, a visionary, a maniac, the antichrist, a hero. Some people said he was dead. Others said he should be but that he was alive, lying in wait to strike. And when he did, the world would never be the same. His plan was to turn Northern Mexico and the Southwest U. S. into an independent new country. He had the men and arms, the drive and the strategy. He was a serious man. Others said he was a serious man all right but only about killing and, thank God, he'd been killed in a bank robbery.

I'd painted his portrait and designed some banners for a couple of his rallies, which he paid for on the spot. That was all the contact I'd had with him. I didn't know if he was criminal or saint, but I was glad he wasn't around.

"Some of Doe's ideas weren't all bad," Vida said as if she'd broken into my brain.

"In many ways, all he wanted was to make a society that worked for all. Like in the Middle Ages where each person had a function and belonged to a body politic which fit together."

She paused to scratch her right breast. I offered. She declined. "You remember the family figures of the man, woman, and child?"

"I orta. I designed that logo for him."

"Well then, you know that everything fit together."

"That'll be the day."

"You're so right." She scratched her left breast. "But it's not a bad idea, even if it is medieval and not very appealing to modern romantics."

I had scant notion of what she was talking about.

"He's not back, is he?" Jake and the Busters were one thing. A run in with Hillman Doe could be serious indeed.

"Not that I've heard." She enjoyed seeing how uneasy I was. "But I hear Carolina's still around."

Carolina, Caroleena, The Sergeant's third and last wife, a sloping mountain of a woman from Mexico, a former whore, a copper presence capable of sending you running, but underneath, a kind, loving woman.

The Sergeant was Hillman's father and dead some time ago. Rumor was The Sergeant did in Hillman's mother in order to marry his second wife, a sixteen-year-old girl. Hillman liquidated his sixteen-year-old stepmother and was sent away to prison. The Sergeant then went to Mexico and brought back the mountainous Carolina. Hillman did his time and returned to kill his father, always keeping a place for Carolina.

The stories were like folktales gone awry. The Sergeant and I had been friends of sorts. I never believed the man capable of cold-blooded killing, although his war stories were of Chateau-Thierry and carnage. He earned a medal and his rank.

He wanted a tomb for his ashes. I cast a statue of him in uniform with rifle and bayonet at the ready.

Caroleena and I had made love once. We found ourselves in a cornfield and it seemed like a good idea. The memory of that passion filled me with an uneasy rush.

"It'll be all right," Vida said. "All I want is a quick ride in that crop duster."

13

Carolina didn't seem to be around, only the pilot. He looked like something out of the old-time funny papers in his thirties aviator cap with huge, dark goggles. He was tall and lined and in no mood to take us up. The wind was swirling. The clouds were growing darker. Our drought looked to be at an end.

I was pretty sure the pilot was Hillman, which made my skin crawl. Then I decided it wasn't him. Hillman was a wanted man and no man would be where he could be found so easily, unless it was true the best place to hide was out in the open.

He pointed to the north and said *No*. Vida laid her unyielding charm on him. Not even Hillman Doe could resist.

So the three of us settled into the two-seater crop duster.

Vida said, "Nice," over and over.

The pilot gave us nice. He set the brakes on the biplane and revved the engine up to an unbearable whine. He let off on the brakes and we went straight up. My belly flattened against my spine. My buttocks bit into the seat. Vida scrooched up against me and laughed. She pointed for me to look down. The earth spun. The pilot twisted off a snap roll, a leisurely barrel roll, and two loop-the-loops.

The winds bounced us about. Vida threw what was left of Miss Betty to them.

Vida motioned down but the pilot wasn't finished. We went into a steep climb that made even Vida turn pale. Then we stalled and fell spinning as if shot down. I thought, We're going to crash, what a goddamned foolish way to die. I promised myself if I got out alive, I wouldn't have another thing to do with Vida Singer.

The ground kept coming up to meet us. I looked at Vida. She hadn't flinched. If she could watch, so could I. I wasn't going to beg. I grabbed a holt of Vida and waited.

The bitter end didn't come. At the last moment, the pilot kicked the engine on and we were on the wing again, which felt wonderful.

We landed and got out. The pilot didn't say a word or smile. Vida looked relieved and happy. I trembled for a minute.

Carolina stood on the back steps and waved. I felt the old warmth return. Vida saw but went on about her business. She gave the pilot a fistful of money.

I told her the coming storm didn't look like a tease, that we'd better get the Hell out or we'd find ourselves stuck in the mud somewhere, if not drowned.

I wanted to go to my place, but she wanted to go back to Miss Betty's. She had a feeling Jake had been messing around where he shouldn't.

The smell of rain was strong. The first drops were as big as marbles. I decided to forget my promise and stick with Vida.

14

Jake wasn't at Miss Betty's and hadn't been. No one had. The place was just as we'd left it. The rain came down harder, with much more on the way.

"Let's get the Hell out of here," I said.

"No. I've made up my mind I want a bonfire." I had never seen Vida look that way.

"You can't." I didn't get a chance to finish the thought.

"The hell I can't."

"Jake'd know."

"Fuck him."

I muttered something about jail and Miss Betty's memory.

"Don't hand me that. I've been in jail before and Miss Betty meant what she said about the past."

"What about all this knowledge?" I felt like a kid trying not to do his first big wrong.

"Let people find their own damn knowledge." Vida looked at the house, the sky, then me. "You don't have to help. I'll do it by myself."

"All that wisdom burned to a crisp."

I didn't do any good. Vida was determined. Her wildness was back in spades. We set fire to the house.

The fire started like it was going to put itself out, but it didn't. It spread slowly, licking at itself. Then it exploded with a rush, cracking and popping. The fire lingered over the frame. It lavished itself on the studs and the roof.

The chickens went crazy. The collies howled. The pigs snorted and became menacing.

Rain drenched everything like a waterfall, but the fire didn't go out. God, what a sight.

"Betty Elizabeth would've liked this," Vida said, soaked to the bone.

I figured we were drowned rats.

15

I didn't have time to wonder what caused the release. I had no idea if it was due to natural order, accident, mischievous gods, or devils at play. For all I knew insects in Latin American caused it, or one too many pieces of junk had been shot into the sky.

I didn't have time to measure the rain, but forty-five and a half inches fell in a twenty-five hour period. We got caught up on our rainfall in a big hurry. A wet meanness replaced the parched dryness.

We made it across one arroyo, but the normally peaceful Leche Quemada Creek with water the color of burnt milk candy cradled a twenty-foot-high wall of water. I listened to the crush and thought, What a terrible music. At no time did I think of a painting.

Vida and I hugged in a *So this is it* anticipation. The roar swamped us and I had the sensation of flying wild like I was long gone. When I came to, I had the pleasant notion I had passed into eternity. It took a second to realize I was alive and in the arms of the mud-peppered Vida Singer. She looked like an alien bird. She smiled and I kissed her.

We were wiping mud off each other and trying to figure out where we were when the helicopter showed up.

My truck had survived but needed work.

The area was devastated. Houses and barns were splintered. Dead animals were all over the place. Gravel trucks and a freight train were thrown about.

The tornado destroyed much of Burro and Causeway, but didn't touch my mother's rest home. A TV commentator described that as a miracle.

Both towns were called heroic. The government declared them disaster areas, an honor, some said, long overdue.

· Vida and I were amazingly no worse for wear. We volunteered for a special search party set up to look for and tally the dead. When we began, twenty-six were known dead, another two hundred were missing. We found seven, all young and naked and dead, drowned on their way to a shelter. Someone said they were washed free from their troubles. Vida said she figured they'd've preferred their troubles.

They looked unreal. Not a sight to linger over.

"I gave you all up for dead," Jake said.

"Sorry to disappoint," we said.

Then he came right out with, "By the way, did you all burn down my Aunt Betty's house?"

Vida looked dumbfounded and I tried to look as blank as I could.

"Later, perhaps," he said.

Vida and I stayed at my place where, for some reason known only to God, I had squirreled away several hurricane lamps, some coal oil and kerosene, a few canned goods, wood, and bottled water. The only damage to the house was a small hole in the roof, which I managed to patch.

I fed and bathed and looked after Vida. She posed for me and we made love in our fashion once or twice. Not a lot of thrashing around, but nice.

A couple of weeks went by and the lights and water came back on and everything was back to normal, including Vida and the truck. I was content, but Vida was seriously restless.

One morning she stepped out of the shower all aglow and said, "Don't understand me too quickly, Wayman, but it's time for me to move back to my place."

She said it so I'd know arguing was a waste of time.

"I have a job of work to do," she said.

Which was a polite thing to say. When I dropped her off, I ached and burned in the pit of my stomach. My teeth felt like ice and my bones hurt. Not new feelings, but hard to get used to.

She kissed me before she went in. I wasn't sure what it meant but I went back to my place without begging. Time to get on with my job of work. I never hated that expression more than at that moment, even if it was best to get on with it.

Part Two

On the Wing

1

The devastation inspired me. I had more energy than I had a right to. I painted my kitchen, a job I'd put off for years. I gave my other work a good lick. A couple of the pictures were solid and good, especially the one of the dead kids. I didn't miss Vida all that much.

I worked around the clock a couple of times. Then one day I had a mild attack of ESP. I hadn't heard from my mother since the memorial service. The phone rang. She wanted to see me muy pronto.

She didn't look any too pleased to see me, even though her preacher friend greeted me with a cobra's smile. My bowels said, punch him in the nose, but I didn't. I could grin too.

"You look good," I said.

She kissed me in a half-ass sort of way. "I don't feel so good."

"I'm sorry."

"I heard you fell on your head in the flood. I assume your memory must be off." She was in good form.

"My memory's okay."

"Folks are saying you've gone off the deep end."

"You know how people talk. I'm no crazier than usual."

"I thought as much." She took a deep breath and looked me straight in the eye. "Sometimes I think I'd just as soon see you dead."

A familiar line from my youth.

"Sorry. I feel better than ever."

"I'm so happy for you."

"Why are we having this dumb-ass argument?"

Preacher Dan looked like he smelled dog crap on the pulpit.

"I don't appreciate talk like that." She looked like a coming squall.

"You all were lucky the storm missed you," I said, trying to ease the tension.

"It was the Lord's will," the preacher said.

"Reverend Daniel sent the tornado elsewhere."

"Oh?"

"Faith," he said, answering my surprise.

Before I could say *No shit* the way young people do, my mother interrupted.

"Everything was coming down all around us. I told everyone to stay calm and do what they were told."

"Your mother was a Godsend."

"I can see that."

"The tornado came like the end of the world. Daniel prayed, the Lord listened, the Lord obeyed." She smiled and grabbed the man. "There was a swooshing sound. The storm lifted. The dark became light. We were spared."

"Praise the Lord," I said. "A miracle."

"Yes, I have a way of seeing sinners punished."

"Oh?"

My mother turned purple. She clenched her fists and made her palms bleed.

"See what you've done," she said.

"What a goddamned fool thing to do," I said.

The head nurse came. My mother's oozing palms weren't a surprise to anyone but me. My mother and her friend did their best to look like saints.

"I have good news for you. Reverend Dan and County Judge Jake are going to help me with my accounts and my will."

"Son of a bitch. A new version of render unto Caesar the things that are Caesar's and unto God the things that are God's."

Reverend Dan looked like the cat enjoying the canary. I could imagine what Jake looked like."

My mother glared at me. "You're never around and to be truthful, you don't know shit about money."

The word coming from her tickled me.

"What'd you mean I don't know shit about money?"

"Just what it sounds like. You know it's true."

It was but I couldn't let on it was.

"The Bible says, honor your mother." My mother's turn to look quietly pious.

"What does that have to do with anything?"

"Just this. You never have time for me. I thought you were dead. You might as well be."

"Goddamn," I said.

"You and your hussy can run off and leave me to die in peace. I'll be all right, now." She gave me one of her motherly-hard looks from my youth.

"Yes, while Jake picks you clean, and Reverend Dan invests your talents."

"Jake's been born again. Don't ever talk that way about Daniel again. He's been in more than one Lion's Den."

Jake born again? I thought stranger things have happened, but not many. As far Rev Dan, as the kids say, he was cool.

"What about your grandchildren?"

"What about them? Like you, they're never around. You're a no good, shiftless drifter. Always have been, always will be, now and forever."

"Is that the new doxology?"

The man reminded me again. "The Bible says, honor thy mother."

"You son of a bitch," I said, louder than I intended. The head nurse heard me.

"Since you're bound and determined to act like a fool, why don't you vamoose?"

I apologized. Before I climbed in my truck, I tried to kiss my mother good-bye. What I got was one of the world's largest oysters spit at my feet.

"Goddamn," I said. I gave her a quick good-bye kiss, winked at The Reverend, and drove off full of admiration. Nobody could spit like my mother. I'd have to decide what to do about Jake and the Rev.

2

The next night a sudden prank of nature changed the weather to an unseasonably drizzly cool. I lay there fighting the sheets and missing Vida's arms around me. I was at such loose ends I got up in the middle of the night and played my prank.

I called the home from a pay phone and did my best imitation of a drunk and lisping Jake. I told the night nurse a bomb had been planted in the home and it was best to get everybody out. Then I drove down. I parked my truck behind a warehouse. I walked two blocks and hid in the brush that ran along a draw behind the convenience store.

Ronnie and his troops came barreling up as did two ambulances and two fire engines from the volunteer fire departments of Burro and Causeway. All that was lacking was the bomb truck from Fort Seneca. There was no shortage of sirens and colored lights.

The firemen strutted around like Mussolinis in the rough. The deputies fanned out with shotguns and drawn pistols. They flashed their lights and muttered threats about what they'd do if they caught the bomber.

They searched the block, but not the block where my truck was. They searched the convenience store and behind it. They gave the brush where I was a lick and a promise, telling each other to watch out for snakes.

Close. After a minute or two, I stood up and watched Ronnie. I knew he couldn't see me, but his tight-lipped grin made me shiver.

The patients emptied out like kids having the time of their lives. That is all except my mother. She looked miserable and gave Ronnie the oozing palms treatment. He turned her over to an ambulance orderly and went about his business. She didn't like that.

She looked for Reverend Dan. He hadn't shown, which made her even more put out.

Ronnie, complete with bullhorn, looked into the TV camera and said. "I want everybody to remain calm. We don't need to wait for the bomb truck. I'm going inside. I know something about bombs. If there's a bomb, I'll find it and personally defuse it. Trust me." I admired his style. He went in like MacArthur.

No bomb was found.

"It's all a hoax!" Ronnie announced. Everybody cheered.

Jake showed up about that time and began throwing his weight around. But the night nurse cut him short and accused him of being the caller. The deputies jumped on him like he was Public Enemy Number One. Ronnie pulled them off and sent Jake on his way.

The residents shuffled back in like cows in a long line. My mother kept looking around like she smelled me.

No real hurt, except the VFDs got into a fight. The ambulances were needed after all.

My mother's preacher man never showed.

Before he left, Ronnie gave the TV camera a last look. "I promise. I'll catch the miscreant (he didn't say bomber or prankster) and bring him to justice."

I got away scot-free.

3

The media had a field day, saying that at long last the people of Sage County had been dragged into the Twentieth Century. How'd they like it?

The rush of the twentieth century eighty years late turned Burro into a firestorm. Strangers poured in. Some came to gawk. Others came to join Vida's new school, full of hope and energy. Emissaries from charities came to save us, the dumb and the deluded.

Gossips had a field day, what with Vida's new school (the woman had not been idle since she moved back home), the infusion of strangers, and my prank.

The joke would not go away. The media linked the scare to dope and terrorism. There was, apparently, a drug-mad terrorist who'd toyed with us, who had us at his mercy. No one was safe in the street, in a public building, in his own home. A hopped-up weirdo could blow us all to Kingdom Come, and there was nothing we could do.

Now was the time to act, to call out the military, to do something even if it were wrong. It was goddamn time to lock somebody up. Somebody had to pay the piper.

Ronnie enjoyed putting the heat on Jake, but he knew Jake hadn't had anything to do with it. But people were restless. The word was Sheriff Ronnie Gilchrist wasn't doing his job.

Which brought him to me. What did I know?

"Nothing," I said.

"You know the FBI has an interest in this."

"The FBI?" My anus closed.

"They don't take kindly to bomb threats, even hoaxes."

"That's good to know," I said.

"Someone told them they were almost positive they saw you high-tailing it away from the scene."

"Not me. I was home."

"I don't know how much longer I can stall 'em. Their need for blood is great. Oh, well, what the hell?" He left.

I'd been involved with the FBI before, when I was a CO. I hadn't liked it.

Ronnie couldn't or wouldn't help, Vida was busy, and whenever I ran into Jake, he just looked at me. I didn't know what to do. So I decided to paint.

4

The first caught the patients lined up in the mist in the dim light with police and reporters all around. A pretty good picture.

The second came out of a sleepless night. Patients were lined up as if they were about to be shot.

The third: The home as an asylum for inmates with bare skulls and wide eyes and lipless mouths.

The fourth was of a few patients frolicking like children while others made love under a tree as the firemen fought. I put Ronnie's face at one end of the painting and mine at the other.

The paintings weren't my best. They helped some, but I still hurt. I had to see Vida. I knew she was busy, but I had to see her. Thank God, she was happy to see me.

"I need a break," she said.

We drove out to the lake and I parked in a private place near the spot I'd come up on Lorrain.

"I have a pretty good idea who the caller is," she said.

"Everybody knows it's Jake."

"Ronnie doesn't think so. Neither does the FBI, and neither do I. What about you?"

"I don't know what you mean. Ronnie's gotten a lot of free publicity."

"Not all of it good. The FBI can be a real pain. They're not all fools." She smiled sweetly. "It's not Jake."

"I suppose not."

"It's not Ronnie, and it's not me. Who is it, you suppose?"

She had me on a spit.

"I don't know." The thought of having to confess made my skin crawl.

She massaged my neck. "How about a swim?"

"Whatever. I don't have a suit."

"Whatever. I don't either." She stripped and folded her clothes in a neat pile.

"No need to be modest on my account," she said.

I debated with myself. It wasn't that I was ashamed of my sixty-five-year-old body. I believed in being careful about when and where to get naked.

Vida eased into the water. "Come on. I don't feel like swimming alone."

We were hidden away and probably safe. I didn't see any curiosity seekers. Still, it took a few seconds before I worked up enough nerve to take my shorts off. Even then, I tried to shield myself as I slid into the water.

The water was almost like a hot bath. A light breeze rustling the leaves helped some. Minnows and small perch nibbled at us.

Sometimes Vida stood up out of the water looking like a great blue heron. Other times she squatted and pulled me to her, holding me tight, kissing me softly. I'd warm to her kisses. A thought would come and she'd get lost and push me away. The thought would leave and she'd pull me back.

She swam with a long, graceful stroke. The best I could do was something between a crawl and a dog paddle. Our bodies didn't look like much, but we felt good against each other.

We had a lot of quiet fun, but our Eden was too good to last. A couple of teenagers parked a discreet distance away. They were soon joined by a patrol car. The kids waved and the officer stared through binoculars that glinted in the sun.

We took our time drying each other off. We got dressed, then drove to my place where we found Sheriff Ronnie waiting.

5

"Have a nice swim?" he asked.

"Yes, thank you. We did," Vida said sweetly. "A body doesn't have much privacy around here these days."

"A body might wear a bathing suit next time," he said.

"Touché!" Vida smiled. "We didn't mean to offend."

"You didn't. Not me anyway." Ronnie looked directly at me. "It seems Jake didn't make that call after all."

"He didn't?" I had a big frog in my throat.

"Are you sure?" Vida asked and put a comforting hand on my arm.

"Pretty much. Enough." He didn't take his eyes off me.

"I see." I wondered why he kept me dangling.

"I don't think you do. Reverend Dan's confessed."

Relief ran out of every pore. "I don't believe it."

"Believe it," he said. "The man's interesting, tender with battered wives and gentle with abused children."

"He's a whiz with widows' finances."

"That too."

"What put you on to him?" Vida asked softly.

"We'd heard stories, so we checked him out. At first he was all you could ask for, then we discovered he was a pornographer. We couldn't believe what we found. So we checked and rechecked. He had it going three ways. He preached against it, he made it, and he sold it." Ronnie fingered the brim of his hat.

"When I asked him why, all he said was, 'The sex isn't harmful if it's gentle. It's the violence that's bad.' One thing, he put the profits in his ministry. I've never had a prisoner like him."

"I can believe that," I said.

Vida gave me a Hush Fool look. "Why do you think he confessed to the bomb hoax?"

It was my turn to give her a Hush Fool look.

"Miss Vida, I don't know why. I've never understood how guilt works. I've never put much stock in confessions. But the FBI's happy, Jake's happy, I'm happy, sort of. I thought Wayman here might be happy too. Case closed, as they say."

"A sad and interesting man," Vida said.

I started to argue but she gave me another Hush Fool look.

"Makes you wonder. He confessed to crimes we have no record of. —By the way, wear bathing suits next time." He laughed. "One more thing, Wayman," the man couldn't hide his shit-eating grin. "Good luck with them pictures."

It took a minute to realize that Ronnie had searched my house. I started to say something, but Vida beat me to the punch.

"You're a good man, Ronnie." Vida gave him a long goodbye kiss.

I was glad to see him go.

"It seems God works in wondrous ways, after all. You're off the hook. Go forth and sin no more."

"I'm a changed man."

"In that case, let's see if we can stir the pot another way. Let's live together without benefit of clergy."

6

Which might not have been the most exciting thing to do in Fort Seneca, but was still hot stuff for Burro. Polite folks said we were having a relationship. Others said we were having a senile affair.

My mother had a bad week, what with Reverend Dan's troubles. —"He didn't fool me. I knew all along he was up to no good." And what with Vida's and my living together. "No matter what you call it, it's living in sin."

But our living together was more than any of those.

We took turns staying at my place, then hers. Once in a while, she'd want to be alone and would wander off. The first couple of times I went looking for her, seeing her sprawled in an arroyo with a broken leg, or bitten by a black widow or a rattler, my heart beating like a bird's. I wasn't sure she meant it, but she knew how to scare me.

Then she'd be back safe and sound, happy to see me. We'd hold each other, sometimes talking all night, other times not saying a word. Laying there, wrapped in her embrace, I thought of nothing else.

Vida seemed to be on the move even sitting in front of her computer. She had no fear of the machine. I promised to learn computer graphics but didn't. I stayed as far away from computers as I could.

Her school grew. People came from all over to listen and learn: Asians, Latins, Arabs, Blacks, Anglos, and all in between. Some of the home folk didn't warm to the new people. They whimpered about a dope-riddled sex factory going full blast in the middle of their once-normal lives.

Vida's school wasn't the only thing to complain about. There were the charities. Those angels did a lot of talking and flag waving, but when it came down to it, they seemed more interested in talking about the good they were going to do than doing it. They were also interested in the pleasures of the flesh.

Finally, Jake got tired and told the charitable folk to zip up and move out. My mother said it proved Jake had been saved. I still didn't believe it.

One nice thing, I was making more money than ever. So much I began to get letters from my ex-wives filled with concern. My children wrote asking about my health and trust funds. I told them I wasn't rich, but the letters kept coming. I was about to drown in a wellspring of affection. I told Dorothy I was going to burn what few paintings I had and hit the road.

She wouldn't let me. She begged for more. I got after it in full stride: Idyllic scenes, storms, people caught unawares; cattle and horses, fields of watermelons and parched corn; Burro's Squared Circle, North Texas faces, North Texas skies; the courthouses in Fort Seneca and Sapient; the separate and always joyfully-decorated-unafraid-of-death Mexican Cemetery. —Latinos were once forbidden burial in Sage's Free Cemetery. Jake had the restriction lifted, but the Latinos, although grateful for the equality, thought theirs more beautiful. They were right.

Then came my Vida series: Vida in her skivvies working her computer with juice in her eyes and a smile on her lips. That poster sold as well as my Mad Betty series.

Vida standing, sitting, reading, thinking, wearing only a large white hat while digging in her garden; naked, front and back, from the side, lying down as if dead, smiling.

Vida, the comeliest of reptiles. Her supple grace and moods were easy to succumb to. I worked with a new passion. I caught her with an edge new to my pictures.

My beloved truck had always been white. I'd been tempted but'd never gone psychedelic. Now I covered it with Vida as a stork, a cat, a python, a woman in the desert, alone in the forest, a woman dominant among man and beasts.

Vida's hugs were a little stronger, her kisses more fervent.

My life was idyllic, yet I felt a tingle. Nothing too strong, only a twitch, perhaps brought on by Dorothy's gushy determination to have, as she put it, a major exhibition of my art.

I didn't see the sense of a fancy show (neither did my mother). All I wanted was my pictures to sell. I didn't get the folderol about how I was better than I knew, how I had put more in my pictures than I imagined, how I'd grown from a hack furniture store painter to something better.

I kept after Dorothy with "Will it sell?" until she knotted up and said, "You bet your sweet ass it will. Why'd you think I'm going to all this trouble?"

I had no comeback. I agreed to the show.

My life was strong and pleasant, yet this small seed kept saying this can't last forever, this isn't you, it's close to time to move on. I told myself if I was anxious, it was excitement about the show and Vida. That and nothing more.

7

There were no flies on Vida. She and her students turned Miss Betty's barn into classrooms and computer labs. They planned new buildings, devised new programs for raising crops and ways to handle stock gentler. They worked on techniques for finding water and saving it, delivering it more efficiently. Their excitement ran so high at times they seemed to be speaking new languages.

Jake told Vida, "Your idea of a seamless society sounds like one of Hillman Doe's pipe dreams warmed over." I wondered if Doe had snuck in the back way. He could have, there were a bunch of new faces, not all of them gentle looking.

I told Vida to watch out, some of the new people could be militia paramilitary, FBI, or terrorists. She smiled and said, "I'll work them and teach them too."

One thing, I was grateful for the time we had together.

She smiled, "Don't look at me like I'm crazy. I like to sit naked in my backyard at night when the weather's nice. It helps me concentrate and plan the day. Feel free."

About the closest I came to feeling free was taking a leak on the hedge that grew around her backyard. It marked the line between Vida's and Jake's lot. I had the feeling Jake liked to hide in the hedge and spy on us. I never caught him. If I had, I'd've peed on him with pleasure. Vida said I better think twice about peeing on a County Judge that had been reborn, who hadn't asked for an apology for the prank call, who said he wasn't going to press charges against us for burning Miss Betty's house down.

I tried to tell her that was all the more reason to worry. I knew Jake and Jake was bad news.

I never caught him and life went on. Dorothy was a bird dog hunting my work. She came up with a Crayola of a misshapen tiger, done when I was six and in Miss Vida Singer's class. It still had a fresh look.

She found a full-length oil of me in my boxing trunks. I looked pretty good. She came across sketches from my CO days, a few from combat, some abstract paintings done after the war, which were better than I remembered.

She didn't ignore my furniture store work: My deer paths, my flower pot still lifes, my gulls, my shrimp boats, my matadors, my Elvises on black velvet, my needlepoint Jesuses, my prickly pears, my hunters, my doves on the wing, my flowers done with a pallet knife. Some folks come over a picture done with a pallet knife: the thicker the paint, the greater the art, the better the bargain. God bless 'em.

She found surrealistic portraits of my wives and a bunch of my nudes. Not as graphic as hers, but they'd sold well. She rounded up a bunch of my dash-'em-off-as-needed Pacific Northwest Mountain and Snow and Stream beauties, my cactuses and the desert and my sunflowers. One or two of my sunflowers went beyond the casual.

I hadn't realized she believed in what she did. I'd always figured she thought everyone was a chump. She wasn't that way at all. She was true. She was thrilled when museums from Fort Seneca, Houston, Dallas, El Paso and New York called. I didn't share her enthusiasm. I had hoped in a half-assed way to avoid it, but the show was going to take place.

8

The last thing to do was my curriculum vitae. It sounded simple enough but when I sat down to write, my feet said time to hit the road.

Vida saw and kept a tight rein on me. We spent nights in her backyard talking and listening to barking dogs, caterwauling cats, the roar of power-packed engines, semis on the highway, the screech of breaks, the now and then crash, the wail of sirens, and squalling tires.

Other times the stillness was broken by the zapping noise of Jake's bug killer. When he forgot to turn it on, we'd be treated to the lights of fireflies and the chirps of tree frogs.

Sometimes the quiet was broken by the sound of organ music, unusual hymns, laughter, a near shriek, and quiet sobbing coming from Jake's. Vida said it sounded like sobbing. I wasn't so sure it was his. I figured it was the youth or Lorrain. I still wanted to catch Jake in the hedges.

Vida said I'd better finish my CV unless I wanted to hear from her.

I played a game. When is a harangue not a harangue, but all the more painful? Answer: When delivered by Miss Vida Singer.

When I did sit down to write I didn't think about my life. I thought about hers. I didn't speculate about her lovers, her Pennsylvania Dutch Men, whoever they were and what they meant. I wondered how many children she had? Were they alive or dead? Had there been none? Had they been stillborn or aborted? Had that crippled her? Not in any way I could see.

She made me think about hate and compassion. She seemed to have stamped quite a few with one or the other. She made me think about the elusive memory of learning. She was a teacher in everything she did. I thought of her knowledge and strength and her love of her, as she put it, classicism (I was still working on what she meant by that), of her unfailed humanity. Not that she couldn't be sharp and hard and mean.

I thought of Mad Betty and her refusal to be crushed, of the vast catalogues I'd helped destroy.

I said, "I can't do it. I agree. Piss on the past."

"Listen to me. I'm sorry we burned Miss Betty's down. I never thought I'd say that. I enjoyed the fire, but now I regret it. I'd take it back if I could. But it's done. —So, put something down so Dorothy can show people what a man the mad artist is."

"I'll make a pact. I'll do mine if you do yours."

"No. Don't ask me again."

I decided to leave that fire alone. I thought of Mexico and wondered if she'd go with me.

"You don't have to stay. You can leave. But I can't. Not just yet." I was convinced the woman could read my thoughts.

"I know I can't walk out on Dorothy." I went back to scribbling. "I'd appreciate it if you'd look this over." I didn't think so, but I said. "It can probably stand improving."

"Let's see." She read a bit and said, "You're right. This can stand improving."

"Thanks," I said. I couldn't believe how mad she made me. I wished Jake and Ronnie were there so I could deck them once and for all. Jake and Ronnie and my mother, anyone from Burro, Causeway, Sapient, Sage County, the whole goddamned world, including Vida Singer and her Pennsylvania Dutch Men, if she liked.

No, not Vida, not really, not yet anyway.

9

The opening was by invitation only. Vida made me invite Jake and Ronnie but said I didn't have to invite any of my ex-wives. My mother, however, was another matter. I had to invite her, that's all there was to it.

My mother liked peanut butter and apricot preserves and apples. So armed and with a drawing of the Scott place and an engraved invitation, I headed for the home.

She hugged me and told me how much she'd missed me, that she'd known all along the Reverend Dan was a crook but try as he may he couldn't dupe her. She told me what a fine son I was, I always had been and always would be.

I gave her the drawing. She hugged it and whimpered like a puppy. She thanked me for the fruit, the peanut butter and the drawing, but not the invitation. She looked at it like I'd offered her a bite out of the poisoned apple.

"I want to tell you something about that woman of yours. She's slept with everybody here and the world over: man, woman, and child, for all I know. We had to run her off. She went out to Hollywood and let them take pictures of her naked and doing all that fucking."

"Fucking?" I laughed.

She ignored me.

"I wouldn't be surprised if she has some disease no one's heard of."

She took a proud breath. "And now she pretends to be so good, so high and mighty, so interested in everyone and everything. Don't let her fool you. She's nothing but a bitch. You'd be better off if she was dead." Her face pulled into a knot. She tilted her head and brushed her hair. It took her a moment to shake out the fury.

"Judge Jake comes by. He asks about you. He's not a sissy like everyone says. He's a nice man. People don't understand what being considerate means."

"They sure don't."

"He wants your forgiveness."

"For what?"

"He didn't tell me."

I wondered what the old fox was up to, but it was time to get to the question that was rattling around my throat.

"Would you like to come to my show with Vida and me?"

"Mister Big Shot," she said with a hard laugh. "Mister Hot Stuff."

"It's not mandatory."

"You should stay with your own people, your own class. You've never lived the way you were raised."

"Would you like to come or not?"

"Only if you and me go to a picture show."

"I have to go now."

"Please stay." She became as coy as a young girl.

"Some other time. I've got work to do."

"Take me for a ride. I want some yogurt." Like a pigeon's coo.

"After the opening."

"Go on then, Mister Bigshot. Go on and leave me alone."

No sense in trying to kiss her goodbye.

"I'll tell Vida you send your best."

She threw the peanut butter at me. I ducked. The jar broke against the wall. She held the invitation and the drawing up to be sure I saw them. She smiled and tore them in two.

I left before it got worse. Her fierceness deserved a memorial. A painting of a giant stinging lizard with her face came to mind.

The good thing was I wasn't going to have to worry about her at the exhibit.

10

The big day arrived. I spent the morning fiddling with my brushes and colors. I fought a mental battle and decided to do something I shouldn't. I found a bottle of gin, the kind that makes your left breast ache, left over from ten years ago when I quit drinking. One reason I hadn't had a drink in ten years was everybody said, "That first drink really knocks you on your ass." During that time I'd never wanted to be knocked on my ass.

The day of the show was different. I mixed that gin with a pitcher of lemonade. The idea was to ease my mind, to reach a plateau of easy grace and serenity.

Time became marble smooth and slow. The sky looked deep and clear and at peace. I drifted into a slow, comfortable float with no topsy-turvy rooms and no spinning ceilings, only sweet softness. I felt disembodied, hypnotized. I heard music. The air was so still the music could have come from miles away. I danced and sang and laughed. I must've made more noise than I realized because soon I heard sirens and cars pulling into my driveway. I listened to engines chugging and dying, to doors slamming and feet stomping as well as shouted instructions. I saw twirling lights and heard bullhorns. I wondered why so many police. Only it wasn't the gendarmes, it was my ex-wives come to rifle my pockets. I smiled. They'd know soon enough how poor I was.

"Get in this house," I said.

The second, the mother of my daughter not mine, looked as young and pregnant as when I met her. I had had the good luck to break down in front of her family's combination home-grocery-filling station one night. She was alone and terrified and helpless and appealing with her young face, her long sandy hair, her big deer eyes and heap of a belly. I fell in love then and there. She didn't bat an eyelash when I asked her to come with me. She was packed and ready to go before I fixed the flat.

She was the loveliest, sweetest girl I'd ever seen. A bastard from the Air Force had tricked her and kept tricking her, promising each time to marry her but never keeping his word. Finally, she took a razor to his testicles one night. He vamoosed, trailing blood and leaving her pregnant and hurting. So, in love and filled with concern, I took her with me and married her, giving her baby my name. That was in 1953, a different time in some ways.

The situation was complicated by the fact that I was already married. Married, but separated from my first, the only one my mother approved of: a hard-nosed businesswoman to be, a bright, efficient, staunch, plump, respectable lady from East Texas, a devout Southern Baptist impenetrably dry in thought, word, and body. I was still young enough at the time to be confident my lovemaking would turn that ice woman into a creature of grateful passion. That the old slippery would loosen that Scotch-Irish shrew up, put a sparkle in her eyes and a devilish smile on her lips. The old slippery, which she accepted as a matter of infrequent duty, never changed her. Her second husband later confided to me she'd become the best browbeater a man could wish for. Yet, that afternoon she was overflowing cheerfulness and had no trouble in taking her clothes off without having to be begged. Neither did my second.

I didn't have two wives for long. The first wanted a divorce because I wasn't much of a moneymaker, which was unholy. The second because I was away too much, the baby needed a steadier, better father.

I was divorced twice in one day, once in deep East Texas in the morning, then in Fort Seneca in the afternoon. I had a lot of energy then. The experience taught me never to underestimate the cleverness of attorneys and the efficacy of money.

I was about to ask them to sit when my third stepped forward, all naked and nubile, grinning as she often did when ready to dive into bed. She still looked nineteen, so much younger than me, a girl of resolute will who wouldn't make love until we were married and who then wore me out in a frenzy of passion; and not only me, but my best friend at the time who she claimed to love more than me and who, after the court identified him as the father of her child, did the right thing by taking her off my hands. Her passion was so intense I ran from her with joy. My friend's cocky smiles soon changed to frowns because her passion turned into a passion for money. At the party, she was all smiles.

I can't tell you how the sight of a woman's sex stirs me to this day. The four of us sat and talked and drank. A very pleasant time was in the making.

It got even better when fat and sassy showed up. Fifty-five, vigorous, bubbly, big breasted, a meld of Czech and Italian blood, she made the air vibrate. She'd been game for anything except my stubbornness and my inability to fit in with her family. So we split. But she hadn't held a grudge. She laughed and gave me a big hug. The world'd never suffer for a lack of energy as long as she lived. What a fertile force she was, giving birth to nine sons in all, two of which were mine.

My lack of orthodoxy was a problem for my fifth, especially when she realized she couldn't convert me. She had a fiery red muff, set off by a white belly and plump white thighs. But she was more in love with sighting the Virgin Mary than making love with me. Without intending to, she gave me the idea of painting pictures of Jesus and the Virgin on barns. I made a few bucks, the barn owners a killing. Miracles and an annulment.

My sixth eased in, a much misused woman from Teochuacan, an earthy saint who could never make her no's stick. Much like Carolina she was too compassionate, too loving for any one man. She went back to Mexico. But she showed up for the party.

Everyone was there, except my children. The boys had always thought I was the problem and didn't come. The girl had grown into a shrewd, aggressive lawyer so bright she might wind up President. I thought of the girl and boy who died so young. I didn't dwell on that emptiness.

Everybody was naked, so I got naked. My exes made a maypole of me. They danced and wrapped me with long ribbons. I lay back and floated and had a good time admiring the power and beauty of my prod. That is, until Dorothy stormed in and chased everybody away.

"I knew it!" she thundered. "I told you, Vida. Just look! Wayman, look at yourself."

I raised my head and looked in the mirror. I didn't think I looked so bad.

"He's pie eyed, that's all," Vida said.

"Pie eyed, my ass! He's drunk as a skunk. And, look at that, would you? Just look at that!"

Vida took a good look. "Maybe what they say about gin is true."

"Give it a good whack. It'll wither up all right." Dorothy was too eager.

"I'll tend to him. You go wait out in the limo," Vida said.

"I hope you give him a good what for. The old goat's got to be half sober. The son of a bitch! Cut if off for all I care. I'll wait but not for long."

Perhaps it was the gin, or the spinning of a spider that made me so ready.

"One nice thing about being a woman," Vida said, "is you can always make love, if you want to." She smiled. "Your chest may be a festival of kerotoses, but you're rather nice down there."

Afterwards, I wanted to sleep, but Vida and Dorothy dumped me in a tub of water so cold I turned blue-ball blue. The two poured hot coffee down me and force-fed me scrambled eggs. I tried to tell them I wasn't as drunk as they claimed.

They did their best to squeeze me into a monkey suit. I rolled up into a knot. That didn't stop Dorothy from pinching and bruising me all over. I still didn't give in.

Finally, she agreed no monkey suit. I put on my pink shirt, my green suit, my orange-brown shoes and white socks. The shoes were scuffed like over-plowed fields but they were comfortable and went with the suit. My old green knit tie fit right in. I topped the outfit off with my yellowing Panama hat. I looked spiffy. I was ready to take on the art world or any other world for that matter.

11

The white limo seemed a mile-long. It had a luxurious red whorehouse interior. I tried to talk to the driver, but he was a big unfriendly sort who rolled the glass divider up. I tried to watch TV, but fell asleep. Vida said my snoring shook the road.

When we arrived at the gallery, Vida held an ice pack against my privates, which woke me up.

Dorothy calmed down when she saw I was under control. She looked good in her best black. Vida produced a peach-orange dress that hung provocatively over her. She was the star of the show. Where I was bumbling, she was smooth, fearless among the sharks. She was oil on the water.

The prime rib, the turkey and the ham, the shrimp and the crab, the avocados and the fruit, the tamales and the beans, the caviar and the salads were all good. Champagne replaced water.

A few of the guests over-served themselves and said what a shame the show wasn't as good as the booze. Dorothy glared them down.

The show was sensational. My pictures never looked better. I felt like weeping.

A prune of a man saw my welling tears. "They are bad," he said through his sweetheart-bow mouth, "But they aren't worth tears." He turned and waddled away with a parting shot, "It's a sin to have the taste I have." I didn't have time to strike back.

A tall guy who looked like an overcooked hot dog sidled up to me. He said he was a well-known, respected art appraiser, with an idea. He would appraise my pictures and give them histories that would be sure to attract wealthy buyers. We would insure the pictures, which didn't sell, at the over-inflated values established by the market and his appraisals. Those pictures would then be stolen or burned, thefts and fires do happen. We would be rich. I thanked him for the thought and moved away as quickly as I could.

A friendly critic said if I'd stuck with my abstract expressionism, I'd be rich and famous by now.

A young woman said I should've stuck with my surrealism.

A tough old bird said he liked my boxing scenes best. He looked like a pug with his knotted brow and flattened nose. He pointed to a picture of a fighter with swollen eyes and blood running down his cheeks. "That's me. You did that to me, then you painted me, you son of a bitch."

"No hard feelings, I hope."

"No hard feelings."

"If it was mine, I'd give it to you," I said.

"No need. I already own it. After you beat me to a pulp, I decided to do something else. I went to work as a roughneck and here I am now, an oilman, the scourge of the earth. How're you doing?"

"Surviving."

"Me too." He grinned. "I'll bet there's not a half a pint of red-hot blood in some of these folks."

I didn't see a lot of red-hot blood, but I'd lived long enough to know the cold-blooded weren't to be underestimated.

"Good luck," he said. "I'll be in touch."

The champagne was good. I had to watch it. I'd had a head start and champagne did strange things to me.

A pear-shaped bald-headed man with a deceptive smile toddled over like a cherub. I made a mental note to introduce him to Jake. At first he looked soft and easy, but the more you looked you wondered why his eyes and mouth were so hard.

He put a hand on me and explained he was a New York art critic, who'd come as a favor to Dorothy, even though "Out of City artists are such a bore these days. They're not hot wired to the center. It's a shame."

I thought, What?

"Dorothy should have called this show Quotidian Banal." For a minute I thought he was talking about a god Jehovah had defeated. He paused to sniff his fingernails.

"What is lacking is an on-the-cusp fury worthy of the now. The artist should try something different, like ejaculating into a condom, then making it the centerpiece. It would speak to life and death in our world of AIDS." He squeezed my arm hard. "He should make a film as well as a painting of the entire process and show them together. An epiphany for the post-modern world, don't you think?"

He didn't wait for an answer. "Who is that little man over there?" He smiled. "I must tell Dorothy how really fine all this is." He squeezed my hand and wandered off toward Jake.

The two left together.

A comfortable lull was settling in when Medea Paresis struck, a bitter freckled woman with small hard tits and tangled hair. She stormed in waving her cane and dragging her frail child-husband behind her on a leash. He panted like a puppy. She let him loose.

I say child-husband. He was my age but plastic surgery kept him baby faced. I didn't believe the stories she diapered him before they went out.

Medea Paresis had been Fort Seneca's artist's artist for forty years. She was an intense, hard-driving person with a reputation for aspirations that exceeded her talent. I wasn't one to judge, but she was a force. She believed art was bad-ass female to the core, that her art had come from pain and agony earned as sweetly as Jesus's.

She called herself Medea Paresis because of her hair and because she claimed to have one of the oldest cases of tertiary syphilis on record. She spared no one she thought a fool her cane.

Dorothy said, "Despite her reputation, Medea Paresis is good at what she does. That's what makes her difficult."

Not my style, but so what?

She scorched me with inflamed eyes and waved her sword at my pictures.

"Pure unadulterated trash! Contamination and pollution. Burning is too good. These need a little laid on action." She waved her cane.

I grabbed her baby-husband by his dog collar and pulled his face close to mine so he could smell the horror of my breath.

"She does anything to hurt Dorothy's show and I'll action paint your nose. Savvy?"

"Fuck you!" he said.

When Medea Paresis saw her Jason in trouble, she charged. Once again, Vida saved me. She grabbed the woman and hugged her. Medea turned into a bowl of sobs. Vida held and Dorothy stroked.

"Yes, Medea, you can have your own show. A woman with your talent and snakes in her hair can't be all bad."

The woman looked reborn. Her husband planted a sawbuck in my hand, with the advice, "Drink a better brand of muscatel and buy a better mouthwash." I thanked him.

Those who stayed to the end looked like bubbles on a wave. They shouted, applauded, and bought. I was filled with love and booze. I let go with a cacophony of popcorn farts.

Dorothy smiled. Medea Paresis beat a tattoo on the floor with her cane. Vida sailed her hat across the room. I grinned, proud of the show and happy I had not shit in my pants.

A reporter called the show an old fart's triumph. I was a hero, albeit a snockered one, a celebrity for a night.

12

I woke up in Vida's bed, feeling a lot hairier on the inside than the outside. I was dizzy and disjointed, my head foggy but not pounding. Deities and devils were not yet kicking things over.

I raised my head. Too much effort, I lay back. I lifted my arms. I lowered them. I lifted my legs. I lowered them. They trembled like leaves. I managed a deep breath. I turned and came face to face with Vida's dressing mirror. I looked like a yellow skeleton dragged in by the dogs.

I became more alert, which was a mistake. I touched my face. It felt numb. I feared the first stage of paralysis. I smacked my lips. They were caked and dry and cracked. My teeth were growing moss. My tongue, that vigorous muscle Vida admired so much, felt burned and dead. I begged the jackals to leave my mouth with their carrion.

I promised reform and good works and perfect behavior if I could raise one drop of spittle. I promised to be nicer to Jake, to my mother. I promised to donate my future paintings to whoever, whatever.

I longed to die, but no such luck. I had to move. The moment I sat up a giant hand squeezed my brain while another pounded drums.

I reeked. I saw fumes rising out of my pores. I thought, Let me die, let the blessing come now, quickly.

"So Pan is alive after all." The soft voice floated in the room. No one likes to admit he hears disembodied voices unless he's an evangelist.

"Does the great Pan feel pain?"

"I don't know about Pan, but I sure do." I rolled over and felt a sharp pain in my left side. A funny bat-like mouse was sucking away at me. I yelled and jumped and slapped the bat-mouse across the room, a serious mistake. My head hurt in a new way.

The disembodied voice took shape. Vida giggled. "It's only your Jew's harp. Don't you remember?"

"No."

She tossed it to me. It was a Jew's harp all right. I hadn't strummed one since I was a boy.

"You wanted a flute but this was all we could find, search as we might."

"I was Pan?"

"Yes, indeed."

"Why do you look so good?"

"Some people are more moderate than others." She grinned. "You don't remember, do you?"

"I remember the exhibit, nothing else."

"Would you like a bite to eat or hair of the dog?"

"Something to eat." The thought of hair of the dog sent spasms through me.

"Sure?"

"Yes."

"You'll have to come to the table."

"All right." I felt the floor with uneasy feet. I looked in the mirror and saw I was naked. "Where're my clothes?"

"Where you left them."

Where you left them sounded like bad news. I smiled a where could they be smile but got no answer. They weren't on the bed or on the floor. It wasn't likely I'd hung them up. I figured Vida sure as hell hadn't. I looked out the window. At least they weren't all over the front yard. They were on the front porch. The cliche I'm too old for this shit was right.

Vida shook her head as if to say, Poor, poor man. I stood up and wobbled. I sat. I stood up again and held it. I'd made it to upright. The trick was to walk.

Vida handed me one of her blue wrappers, which protected what was left of my dignity.

I opened the screen door and stepped onto the porch. The sunlight hit hard. I smiled and stretched to show the neighbors there was nothing to get excited about.

Bending was an adventure but I managed to pick up my clothes.

Back inside, I asked, "What happened?"

"You better eat first."

"That bad? —Where's your things?"

"I'm a tidy person. I hung them up."

"Was I the only one . . . ?"

"You were not alone." Vida said gaily. "I behaved myself. Dorothy and the chauffeur were another matter."

"The big black guy?"

"The big black guy. He was shy at first. Don't you remember?"

I was as dry as hard baked clay. I didn't want to pursue the conversation. "What about some orange juice?"

Vida looked skeptical. "Okay."

I was just about to tell her I never vomited when the juice hit bottom, turned around, and headed back up. I made it to the commode in the nick of time. I hugged the commode as best I could.

13

I can't say enough against the dry heaves. Finally, I was able to take a bath, although climbing in and out of the tub was tricky. The world smelled better and so did I.

Shaving was another problem. I thought, Why shave again? My whiskers would be white and soft and hide my chin and neck. I'd look grandfatherly, Godlike, serene. I studied my reflection. I decided one bearded God was enough. I shaved carefully, very carefully.

A quiet flow of energy suggested I was going to live after all. I lay down and slept until Vida woke me to say supper was ready. The smell of pan-broiled T-bone and baked potato reminded me how hungry I was.

"So, tell me, what happened?" I said as I sat down to eat.

At that moment the hairs on the back of my neck stood on end. I was no mystic, but I knew what was about to happen.

"That'll be the Sheriff," I said.

"You do remember," Vida said.

"Not completely."

"I don't believe you."

It was Ronnie right enough, with a nervous young deputy.

The two came right on in. "Want me to search the place?" The deputy danced as if he had to pee.

"You have a warrant?" Ronnie asked.

"No, but we're inside and there has to be probable cause, doesn't there?"

The kid made my stomach wince.

Ronnie ignored him.

"Should I cuff 'em?"

"No."

"Should I arrest them, then cuff 'em?"

Ronnie turned to Vida and asked, "You have a Holy Bible in this house, Miss Vida?"

"In the living room bookcase."

"Son, you go in the living room, take that Bible out of the bookcase without breaking anything, sit down without breaking anything and read Matthew, Chapters Five, Six and Seven. There will be a test." Ronnie managed a smile, but his eyes showed little humor.

"I saw these people out at the lake and Judge Williams . . . "

"Please, son. Do as you're told."

The boy looked puzzled but obeyed.

"Won't you all join us? We have enough to feed an army."

"No, thank you, Miss Singer. Strictly speaking, this isn't a social call."

"What is it then?" I said with more snarl than intended.

"Surely you must know, after last night."

"We were expecting you," Vida said.

"What about last night?" I said, still testy.

Vida gave me a clear, unmistakable Shut the Fuck Up! look.

"A good question." Ronnie rubbed his chin almost playfully. "About last night? Where to begin?" He scratched his head.

"Mind if I have a glass of that ice tea?"

"Certainly, Sheriff. Pardon my bad manners." Vida poured him a glass. "Lemon?"

"No, ma'am."

"Sweetener?" She held up a fruit jar full of a dark liquid that looked like honey but was rum.

"A smidgeon," he said.

"Say *when*." She poured.

"When." He raised his glass. "Here's to it." He took a healthy swallow. He smacked his lips and said, "Good tea," and not a word about Sage being a dry county and how we shouldn't be serving alcohol even in the privacy of Vida's own home.

"Would your deputy like a glass?"

"He wouldn't appreciate the subtleties, ma'am."

We smiled.

"I'm sorry I missed your show, Wayman. Maybe someday you can paint a picture of me on my horse."

"I'm better at cows," I said.

"Wayman'll be delighted to paint you on your horse. He seldom has such a subject." She smiled at Ronnie and flipped me off with her eyes. She enjoyed being free with my time.

"Thank you, Miss Vida," he said. He looked at me. "It's a deal then."

"It's a deal." I hoped Vida had kept us out of jail, but for what I didn't know. I was hungry but waited.

"Rumor has it Jake has an incurable disease and is being treated by a faith healer in Wells."

"I'm sorry for Jake," Vida said.

"I didn't come here only to talk about Jake."

"I supposed not," Vida said. "What can we do for you?"

"I guess we might as well start with the day you all went skinny dipping."

"We didn't hurt anybody," I said.

He looked at me like I'd be a lot better off if I kept my mouth shut.

"I hear a lot of stories about Wayman here urinating in the yard."

"An old man can't always make it to the privy." I tried to make it a joke.

He did grin some. "In this county the urinating isn't the problem. You can urinate on the street at high noon as long as you don't expose your genitals. Exposing your genitals is against the law, not the taking of the leak. That's the law, no matter how funny it sounds." He smiled and looked like he was more ashamed than anything. "I'd much rather hunt down a killer than have to talk to you all like this."

"It's hard to see the harm," Vida said.

"Wayman's pissing is not the problem. Neither is the marijuana. They're pissant."

My time to cut my eyes at Vida. She'd never said a word about marijuana to me, never smoked in my presence. I wondered how many other secrets she had and that scared me. I told myself I didn't have to know everything she did or had done.

I said, "I smoked marijuana once in a village outside Mexico City and had nearly got thrown in jail." That made no impact at all.

"Like I say, the marijuana's pissant."

"What is it then?"

"They say you're a threat to the county, that you're planning a revolution or some such."

"For the life of me, how can that be? We don't have a cache of illegal weapons. We don't go around shooting people."

I'd never seen her angry in that way before.

"No, ma'am, you don't."

"What is it then?" she asked softly.

"As near as I can tell, it's fear of the school. Parents are afraid you're going to steal their children, change their lives."

"That might not be a bad idea, but it's pure poppycock."

"Last night didn't help."

"It was a small celebration. Not a very wicked one," Vida said.

"The way I get it," the Sheriff in Ronnie said, "Wayman, here, led a rather unusual dance in the front yard. A dance topped off by two people making love. These two people being a very large black male and a very large white female."

Goddamn, Dorothy and that black man. Of all the things to see and I'd missed it. Dorothy and the black man. No wonder everybody was up in arms. It wasn't the noise and our bare asses. It was race and fucking. We were lucky we hadn't been lynched.

"That story's not true, Ronnie, and you know it," Vida said softly but firmly.

"Wayman's clothes were in the yard, weren't they?"

"On the porch." She could be so conciliatory.

"And the neighbors complained, didn't they?"

"Not to me, they didn't."

"Vida, Miss Singer, I didn't come here to argue over the details of last evening."

"I'm not arguing. Am I arguing, Ezekiel?" She sounded like my mother.

I was still working on images of Dorothy and the chauffeur.

"No matter. I'm here as the Sheriff and a friend to tell you there's talk of having you two committed."

"On what ground?" I asked.

"Insanity," he said.

"Do you think I'm insane, Sheriff?"

"No, ma'am, I don't. But what I think don't always count." The man hung his head, then looked at us.

"Let me play the Devil's Advocate. From their point of view a lot of strange things have happened in a short period of time. Miss Betty's death, her memorial service . . . "

"The people didn't think we were crazy then," I interrupted.

"Not the same people. I'm talking about a group with a different sort of power. A group that gets scared of its own shadow. —But to continue the list. The fire, the bomb scare, the skinny dipping, Wayman's pissing, Miss Vida's walking around naked, the dance last night. I could go on."

"Please do," she said.

"The marijuana, the fear of the school. People don't mind eccentrics up to a point. But if they think the eccentric has quit being an eccentric and become a menace, that's a different ball of wax."

"Do you think I'm a menace? Are you here to arrest us after all?"

I'd never seen Vida that serious. My skin went to gooseflesh.

"Not this trip, but I'm running out of room. I don't want to lock everybody up like my deputy in there does. I like my jail empty. Which isn't to say I can't come down hard. —Some more tea, please."

The man took half of it in one gulp.

"By the way, Zeke, you look real fetching in that wrapper. You take to wearing women's clothes and you will be in real trouble." He let a wicked grin crawl across his face real slow.

"I meant it about the picture," he said. Then he looked at Vida with what could only be love.

"Better I say these things to you, Miss Vida, than others. You're a great lady. God broke the mold when he made you."

"I take that as a compliment."

"There's a bunch of unfriendly folks out there right now."

"I know. Wayman and I don't mean to scare the young, or the old." She stopped and looked him full in the eye.

"Your father and I were very close at one time. Like you, he was a good man."

"Yes, ma'am, I know."

"I was there when he died."

"So I'm told."

"You might say he died in my arms."

"So I hear," he said.

"Be careful what you believe when folks gossip," Vida said.

"Yes, ma'am, I know."

They collected the deputy.

"You finish the assignment?" Ronnie asked.

"Yes, sir, I did."

"You understand it?"

"Yes, sir."

"Well, I wish I did, especially the part about judging."

Vida walked them to the patrol car. She shook hands with the deputy and said, "Ronnie, you never did say if you thought I was a menace. Do you?"

"I think you could be if you wanted."

She laughed and kissed Ronnie long and hard. She waved as they drove off.

When she came back in, she said, "Sheriff Gilchrist is almost Christ-like at times."

She'd never said that about me. I didn't like it. That and my supper was cold.

14

We were in bed touching, letting each other know we were there. It was nice and quiet and peaceful. I'd about decided the story of the coupling in the front yard was gossip mongering. Even so, it was time to swear off alcohol again.

Giving up booze would be easy. But other matters began to eat on me until I couldn't leave well enough alone.

"What was that about Ronnie's old man dying in your arms?"

"It's true," she said.

"Were you his nurse?"

"Among other things."

"What'd he die of?"

"I'm not really sure. Heart attack, cerebral hemorrhage, love. Who knows?"

"He was in your arms?"

"He was in more than my arms if you must know."

I didn't say a word.

"Does that make you jealous?"

"Yes."

"Anyway he died in my arms. All my other lovers have gone their merry ways no worse for wear."

I hit the bed hard.

"Don't let it bother you. Just think how jealous those Pennsylvania Dutch Men would be if they knew about you."

I thought, Damned small consolation.

"Go to sleep. Enjoy your triumph."

I couldn't.

"You mustn't believe everything I tell you," she said.

I balled my right hand into a tight fist.

She held it and rubbed it against her chin.

"Such tension," she said.

I tried to laugh it away, without luck.

"You were pretty good at fisticuffs, weren't you?"

"Once upon a time."

"Your self-portrait reminded me. It's an excellent picture."

"It has a lot of the amateur's enthusiasm."

"Don't belittle yourself." She stroked my fist. "What a pretty animal you looked in your boxing trunks. We were all certain you were going to be champion of the world."

"So was I. Me and Traber Hawkes."

"I think I slept with that boy when he was a boy, which was one stated reason I got run off, either the second or third time. I forget which."

I didn't go to the trouble of asking who hadn't she slept with.

"Traber was lightning fast and a great puncher. He was going to be heavyweight champion of the world and I was going to be king of the light heavies. We were going to be rich and famous and have a mile-long trail of women at our beck and call." The memory hurt.

"We did all right for a couple of country boys until Traber broke that guy's neck with one perfect left hook."

"Most nearly perfect," she said. "Nothing's perfect. Most nearly perfect. Repeat it."

I thought this was a hell of a time for a grammar lesson, but I repeated "Most nearly perfect."

"It was one beautiful punch, part of the game, but Traber didn't see it that way. He fought a few more times and let himself be pounded into hamburger. Then he went home one night, laid his pecker out on the carving board and chopped it off. And that was that for Traber."

"I heard," she said. "Sad."

I started to ask who for? Love was making me jealous of the past.

"I swore I'd win both titles, but the war came along and changed all that."

"Yes. I was off teaching or making funny blue movies or roaming the hills when you announced you'd become a conscientious objector. Not every day the number-one contender for the champeenship turns CO. You were fortunate they didn't hang you."

"A lot of people wanted to. Hardly anybody believed me."

"I believed you. I have never taken revelation lightly."

"I don't know if it was revelation or not. I didn't see any bright lights or hear a voice from above. But one day the thought was there. We shouldn't be killing each other, even if God was on our side. I became a CO. I was very young."

"Yes, but maybe you were right," she said.

I felt warmer than ever towards her. "No matter. I wound up in the army anyway."

"What made you change? Were you faking after all?"

"I may have been, but I don't think so."

"The pressure must've been tremendous." Her voice softened.

"There're always loudmouths and hardheads."

"Don't I know?" She laughed.

"I learned a lot as a CO. I did a lot of hard work. I cleared trees, dug ditches, and even looked after the insane for a while. Then I was put in with a bunch of college boys who read and argued a lot about fate and life. Poor souls, they couldn't help feeling superior."

"Did you beat them up?"

"No, all I did was grow a red beard. A couple of them said I looked like a cross between Eric the Red and Jesus Christ. They wanted to crawl into bed with me because I had such empathy for mankind. I decided to join the fight. But not because of that. I just didn't belong there."

"You were decorated, weren't you?" She pushed at me like teasing a snake.

"Yes."

"For killing a hundred of the enemy."

"No, not that many. Only three." I thought how funny the *only* sounded.

"I heard it was at least a hundred." As if I was lying.

"No, three."

"Can you tell me about it?"

"I'd been assigned as a behind-the-lines staff artist, which wasn't bad duty, but I was bored. So one day, I commandeered a jeep."

"Commandeered? You mean stole?"

"No," I said laughing, "I commandeered this jeep to go on a joy ride. I wound up in a village so bare there wasn't even a cat in sight. I got out to sketch the fountain, when I heard a funny kind of chimes. Bullets pinging off stones. Three German soldiers were shooting at me from a roof across the plaza. I used to wonder if they were bad shots or trying to warn me off. Anyway, I shot each of them in turn."

"I see," she said softly.

"I got the silver star, a medal from the village, a kiss from the mayor, a little drunk, and maybe some contraband nooky. I don't remember."

"Sure you don't."

I ignored that. "For a while I wore a hair shirt, thinking I'd killed a form of the Trinity."

"What made you change your mind?"

"I remembered what my company commander told me when I got to France.

"'I hear you're an idealist of some sort.'

"'No sir, not me, sir.'

"'Well, I hope you aren't here to fight for God, Mother, Country, the Human Race, or Apple Pie.'

"'No sir, not me, sir.'

"'Because if you are, you'll be dead before you can say Fucking Jack Robinson.'

"'What should I fight for, sir?'

"'Your buddies and yourself. Especially yourself. If that's not enough, you'll wind up goddamned dead in a goddamned grave somewhere.'

"Not a thing about, Greater love hath no man or the Golden Rule. It was sometime before I was even halfway comfortable with his advice. But I did get rid of my hair shirt."

She stiffened and sat up straight. "Did you hear that?"

"Hear what?" I was still in Europe.

"Someone's at the back door. Go see who it is."

"I didn't hear anything."

"Listen!"

I heard. The knocking was almost a pounding. I feared Ronnie'd come back. I put on a pair of trousers and a pair of old house-shoes. Not that it mattered. It was only Jake in his pajamas, standing there all bleary eyed.

"What'd you want?"

"People are no damned good," he said.

I started to thank him for that wonderful insight and close the door in his face. But I saw he had been doing some hard crying. I opened the door and let him in.

I pointed for him to sit at the kitchen table.

"Breakfast?" I asked.

He nodded.

"Bacon and eggs all right?"

"Whatever's easiest."

"Ain't nothing easiest," I said.

The man was a wreck. I'd never seen him that way. I'd wanted to many times, but now that I did, it wasn't as much fun as I'd imagined.

I put a glass of orange juice in front of him with a multiple vitamin, some vitamin C with Rose Hips, a B complex vitamin, vitamin E, and a digestive enzyme pill.

"Good for you," I said, taking mine. "Hold that one until after the meal."

"What is it, cyanide?"

"If it was I'd say take it now. It's a pill to help old folks digest."

"Can't hurt," he said, swallowing the juice and the vitamins with a shiver. "Orange juice always gives me goosebumps."

"Jake, old sod, I'd like to do a picture of you just like you are now. It'd be a good one." I wondered what was taking him so long to get to the trouble.

I asked Jake as a joke if he cooked, made or fixed breakfast. He didn't say. All he did was look depressed. Then it dawned on me the man had come to apologize for siccing the Sheriff on us, but he didn't. All he did was sit. Maybe that was enough.

The smell of biscuits and eggs and bacon and redeye gravy was hard to resist, but the man didn't eat. Not even when I pushed the plate under his nose.

I gave up. "Have a fig." I ate one and felt an immediate flow of energy. "Figs and mangos are the two principal arguments for the existence of a benevolent creator."

The man was in no mood for such humor.

"I went to see your show again. It's very good," he said.

"I appreciate that," I said, a shade snotty.

He looked around the kitchen as if cataloguing the red and yellow oilcloth on the table, the hanging light, the slightly orange walls, the small pictures (none of which were mine), the old porcelain white stove with iron skillets sitting on the burners, and the new burnt-orange refrigerator which looked out of place.

"You haven't taken a bite of your breakfast," I said.

The man stood up, looked at me for a moment or two, then said, "I'm not perfect. All I try to do is keep a rein on things so no one gets hurt too bad. That's all I do. Thanks for breakfast." He left.

"Goodbye, Jake," Vida said.

"How long have you been there?"

"Long enough."

I scraped his breakfast into the trash.

"He's fixing to destroy himself," she said. "Poor man."

"Nonsense. Not Jake. He's too selfish."

"Maybe you'd like to spend a couple of days at your place," she said.

"Sure. I'll wash the dishes, then we'll go."

"I meant by yourself."

"Better yet," I said, wondering what had set her off. I deliberately broke Jake's plate, pretending it was an accident.

15

A couple of days alone would do me good. All the time in the world alone wouldn't be all bad. I'd have time to catch up with myself and do a picture of a ripe fig. Vida could strut and do whatever she wanted. She and her pupils could march on Burro for all I cared. The sight of her and her bunch of ragtags would rub more than a few nerves raw.

Maybe she wanted to count her money. She had to be raking it in what with all the growth.

Could be her Pennsylvania Dutch Men were coming to town and Miss Vida, savior of the world, wanted to be alone with them so they could screw and dope up.

I was ashamed of that thought. Vida could be a self-righteous know-it-all, but usually not. She was old and contrary, but you didn't have to be old to be contrary, all you had to do was be encouraged.

Vida was right about a good many things but not about Jake. Fat chance he was going to kill himself, he was too fond of his grip on the county. Then too, he had us and his two slaves to rag.

If Jake was acting strange, it was because he was goddamned well aware of what he had done to Mad Betty and Vida and me. Nothing wrong with Jake save a multitude of unrepented sins he was proud of.

Vida was wrong. Mother Jake wasn't about to kill himself. And if he were, I'd be the last person he'd come to for help.

So I went home to my stone house, damn near to dotey. Feeblemindedness and senility looked to be right around the corner waiting for me, while Vida was fresh, eternal, primeval.

The two days became a week.

I went to see Dorothy, who was glad to see me but wouldn't talk about what happened after the opening. She lined up a radio interview for me. A newspaper wanted to talk to me and public TV wanted me for a panel. None of which was my cup of tea, but I did them, even though more and more I felt I should be moving on.

I went to see my mother, who was so glad to see me she clammed up good and tight like a stubborn child. She turned purple and fainted. I caught her as she fell. No sooner had she come to than she saw me and clammed up again, this time turning a deeper shade of purple. A big horse of a nurse got a belly full of that real quick. She held my mother with one arm while with the other she pulled the old lady's panties down and set her on a block of ice. My mother opened her mouth all right then.

She couldn't do her trick anymore, but still wouldn't talk to me. She went out of her way to talk to everybody else, even those she didn't like, being polite and friendly and jovial as could be. I stayed there for a couple of hours without her saying a word to me. What a gift for anger!

I wanted to see Vida. I didn't want to do anything but see her.

I figured she was low on groceries so I stopped and bought three bags full, all for the lady who lived down the lane.

16

I let myself in the back way and called out. No answer. I called, "Anybody home?" Again, still no answer. I feared the worst. My heart pinched.

I tiptoed into her sanctuary. My heart relaxed. There she was, well and radiant and packing.

"I don't remember ordering any groceries, young man. But since you're here, you may as well put them in the kitchen."

"Yes, ma'am."

"For you," she said, tipping me a dollar. "I'm sorry it isn't more." She let her hand linger in mine. "You have strong hands, young man."

"Vida."

No answer.

"Miss Vida."

"Yes."

"It's me, Wayman."

"Oh, yes, you thought I didn't recognize you." She said like a young girl playing at being fey.

"Yes."

"I tricked you, didn't I?"

"You sure did."

We hugged each other.

"Enough of that. I have to finish packing."

"Where're you going?"

"To the West Coast. You know the line, 'I used to be in pictures?' Well, I was. The Pacific should be good for my health."

"What about your school?"

"I have schools all over."

"The one here."

"The students no longer need me. They can teach themselves now." She grinned. "I have friends all over. I can start one out there."

"When are you leaving?"

"The next day or so. Soon, there's no hurry." She gripped me like a bear. "God, I've missed you. Where have you been?"

"I've missed you," I said. "Please don't start in on me."

"You'd like that, wouldn't you?"

"Yes, I would. I surely would."

17

We sat in the backyard fully clothed, talking and looking at the darkening sky, hoping to see a shooting star before the clouds took over. Vida kept coming in and out of the past until thankfully she settled in the here and now.

"You should go visit Jake," she said.

"Jake doesn't need me."

"How's your mother?"

"More determined than ever."

"Good for her." Vida laughed. "I'm serious about leaving."

"I'd miss you."

"There's nothing more for me here."

"I wish you'd stay."

She smiled at that.

"Want me to come with you?" I asked.

"Later."

"I could drive you."

"Let's not argue. Let's not spoil our marriage of convenience. All right?"

"Perfectly all right."

"I do love you." She put her left hand over my lips. I didn't say a word.

That night, stretched out beside her, scarcely touching her, I thought I loved her but how aggravating and exasperating she could be. Perhaps she should strike out and see how far she'd get. She'd fry her brains or freeze to death. She'd learn who cared.

A spasm of nervous energy shook me. Here I was trying to keep her from leaving when inside I kept hearing, I need to move on.

Another shiver. No matter what I felt about me, it seemed best for her to stay. The trick was finding a way to keep her from going. I could tell Ronnie and Jake the great Miss Singer had jumped the tracks and gone off the deep end. She had finally lost it. They would see it. She would be institutionalized for her own good.

Would not be easy, Vida wouldn't submit without a fight. But what if she surprised everybody and said All right? What if she sat right down, and died? Like it was nothing more than snapping her fingers.

A goddamned miserable thought.

I rolled over. Why punish myself? I did my best for her in every way I could.

I always did my best—in everything. Like when I painted those murals of plump women for a Galveston whorehouse at the same time I did a stained glass window for the local Christian Church, a smiling Jesus looking down on the congregation.

Like when I designed the cover for a phone book. Mercury was naked with a banner covering his loins. But peeking out from under that banner was his hard-to-see-at-first uncircumcised member. That was my last phone book jacket.

Vida whimpered. "I'm here," and a gentle shake soothed her. She muttered "Bad dream of all things," and went back to sleep.

She wasn't crazy or senile. The threat of confinement wouldn't work. And, thank God, Vida wasn't about to lay down and die.

I rolled back over. The woman was precious, and knew it. An appeal to her vanity might work, but she would say I was a foolish old man full of sentimentality, that she would go to California alone if she damned well pleased.

I snuggled up against her and kissed her between her broad shoulders. I was so caught up in her I didn't hear the shot. But she did.

"That's it," she said. "Didn't you hear it?"

"I didn't hear anything." And I hadn't, not a backfire, not a firecracker, certainly not a shot. "You were dreaming again."

"Jake's gone and done it. I know." She got up. "Coming?"

"Jake hasn't shot himself. You had a bad dream."

"Coming or not?"

"All right. Coming,"

Vida was right. There had been a shot. When Jake was a kid, he used to suck on a pistol and pull the trigger, then laugh at the click. Some joke. I told him one day he'd forget to unload. This time he hadn't unloaded.

18

Jake did not die a spectacularly rich man. Folks figured he had skimmed millions but only a little more than a million and a half turned up here. Not too shabby but not what was expected. Gossip was he had much more hidden offshore and in Third World Countries.

He left a goodly amount to Lorrain and the boy. They disappeared. People expected to find their remains any day.

Jake's will was different. He maintained he had not taken or stolen money or property from the people (which wasn't completely true), that he would have negotiated with the Devil for the good of Sage County, Texas; The United States of America, even the world. He said a man in politics had an obligation to look after himself, else how could he serve, but what he had done, he had done for the benefit of the people.

He said death would not stop progress, that people were no damned good, the benefit of which was they would survive better than they had any right to. He had the faith.

He asked forgiveness for having wronged Miss Betty and Miss Vida, even though it seemed a good idea at the time.

He left me ten thousand dollars to do a portrait of him to be hung in the courthouse at Sapient.

He confessed he'd always loved me, that as a boy he often sat outside my house just to be near me.

I was not to flatter myself. I was not the reason for his suicide, neither was anger or guilt or sickness.

He left a short poem:
> *This is the thing to do*
> *Don't feel blue.*

I admired his humor. I didn't feel blue at all.

19

Jake's burial was sumptuous. The Busters outdid themselves.

My mother said she would not attend the funeral of a man who had committed suicide. Everyone else, however, who was anyone, turned out.

Sage County had never seen so many sleek limos with long-legged platinum blondes whose funeral attire looked like black lace shortie pajamas and stylish men with the elegance and touch of well-muscled fops. Both boys and girls were tanned to the point of cancer and wrinkles. The big-boy politicos looked their usual selves.

Vida was elegant spidery grace. I was a mournful pallbearer in a dark suit Vida made me buy. I'd wanted to rent it.

The eulogies were overblown sweet.

It wasn't true Jake was buried face down. I did not do a Pan dance on his grave. Neither did Vida void on it. We stopped on the way home so she could relieve herself on the savannah.

"You know, Wayman, some of the best blue movies feature shots of women urinating."

"Interesting," I said, on the lookout for the law.

She straightened herself. "Did you hear who said 'So much for Jake'?"

"I didn't hear anyone."

She eyed me. "They said it there at graveside."

"Wasn't me."

"Sometimes, I feel so old." It was as close to self-pity as she'd come. "Most of the time I feel like I'm thirty-two. I feel, I imagine, I see what to do then a cog slips. I look in the mirror and see my age. I don't mind mirrors the way I did when I was fifty. It took a while to work out of that." She laughed.

"That's one of the good things about your paintings. You show the splotches and loose skin, but that isn't all. I don't mean you're sugary or sentimental, or that you make me a saint. But you bring something to me." She smiled.

"How hard it is to . . . ." She became silent. Everything about her seemed final.

She got up and went to the bathroom. I heard water running in the tub. She turned off the water and yelled, "I've decided not to leave. Not just yet." I felt a lot better.

She came out naked, "Mustn't scare the children." She handed me a towel to dry her back. She kneaded at herself. "I seem to have developed a rash. See."

She looked like she'd been bitten by mosquitoes and chiggers, but it wasn't mosquitoes or chiggers or spiders or stinging lizards or bee stings. It was good old-fashioned poison oak and poison ivy, except there was nothing good about it.

She swole up. Strange looking goop oozed out of blisters and crusted over. The itch must've been agonizing. I would've torn at myself, but not Vida. She said she wouldn't and she didn't.

Her face disappeared under the swelling, both eyes crusted shut. A sight so unusual you had to bite your tongue to keep from laughing. She had become a different sort of ugly funny.

The only ones she let treat her were me and Esperanza. Esperanza was new at the school, a young doctor up from Mexico, rumored to be Hillman Doe's lover. Her nose was like a broken finger. Her dark eyes and wide white toothy smile brimmed with energy. Her feet were big and bony and struck the ground hard when she danced.

She had a fine rear end and a bigger bosom than she cared to show. She couldn't have been more than thirty, but she was a force.

She had a flair for medicine. She taught nutrition and cleanliness, midwifery and human sexuality at the school. She was the kind of woman you could love without hope of being loved in return.

With her illness, most people seemed to have changed their minds about Vida. They didn't come as buzzards. They meant well and left either food or a remedy.

Some offered the offending leaves, saying the way to be cured was to eat them. Others brought goat's milk for Vida to bathe in. Someone left a case of homemade salve, made from God knows what. Two brothers brought jars of brownish clay.

An old woman donated a gallon of cow's milk laced with herbs to be drunk. A shy, rawboned old farmer left a Number 3 washtub full of horse urine. He guaranteed Vida if she bathed in it, she'd be cured *muy pronto*. A spirit-filled church conducted prayer vigils, which Vida supposed might be less effective than the horse piss.

"I feel like a sideshow. What's happening to me?"

Esperanza said she was having a severe reaction to the sap in the leaves and asked if she'd ever had such a reaction before. Vida heaved and said, "Piss on the past." Esperanza laughed and tried again. Same result. Esperanza looked to me. All I could do was shrug.

Esperanza said Vida should go in the hospital. Vida said she'd die first, a reply we took as a good sign.

But no matter how clear and firm and hardheaded Vida was, we weren't convinced she was going to recover.

Esperanza smiled. "Miss Vida, how about a steroid shot or two?"

Vida said, "I'd rather bathe in horse piss."

"That can be arranged," I said.

"Have at it."

One of the hardest things I've ever done is hold Vida while Esperanza gave her the shots. The treatment turned out to be worse than the illness, which is saying something.

The shots were stopped. I continued bathing the woman with cool water and lotions, but my hands and techniques were not always gentle.

Fortunately Lorrain and the boy showed up alive and kicking, full of stories about their splurge and pleasures new to them. Vida was happy to see them, but she required the patience of Job from me.

And my patience was none too good. The way she twisted, the way she sighed, the way she tensed, was almost sarcastic. All I did was rub against the grain every now and then.

I daubed at her eyes and lips. She nipped at me. I felt like shaking her.

"You ever think about your funeral, Wayman?"

"You ever think about yours?"

"No," she stormed and sat straight up. Her eyes popped open. She was suddenly on her way back. The medicine and the bathing hadn't hurt. She looked at me and joked, "I am healed."

20

Vida became friskier while I sagged. Esperanza suggested I disappear for a few days, go some place where I could relax, recharge my batteries, even, she said, restore my soul.

I wasn't sure what state my soul was in, but I needed to get away for a while. An opportunity had come my way.

The oil-man-boxer had bought The Gentlemen's Club in Fort Seneca and wanted me to paint some murals, to do a poster or two, and to slap some paint on a few billboards, if that kind of work wasn't beneath my dignity now.

The project would take only a week or so, the pay would be more than good. I could come out of my ivory tower. I could get sweaty again.

The life had gone out of my paintings. The portraits of Jake and Ronnie were like formal funerals. Whatever Ronnie was, he was life. Whatever Jake had been, he was life. I needed the job. I needed to be in the commercial world again. The only hitch was I was afraid of what Vida might say.

She might say I was deserting her, ruining what talent I had, that I was losing my self-respect, that I had no business lending my name to such a club. She might say that to go was to be a traitor to myself, to her, to Mad Betty. I could hear her saying, "Don't come crawling back to me begging forgiveness. It won't do you any good."

I stood there shaking as I told her.

She looked me in the eye and said with a smile, "That sounds real good, Wayman. A change will do you good. I know you're at loose ends. Go on. Have a good time. Come back when you're finished. There'll be plenty to do here."

She gave me a kiss and teased me about the times I accused her of faking how sick she'd been.

I was disappointed she didn't plead with me to stay, but her eyes showed she'd miss me, and that made me feel good.

She'd be all right. Lorrain and the boy and Esperanza wouldn't let anything happen to her. They knew where to reach me. Anyway, Vida was stronger than fire ants. She'd be all right.

Everyone wished me well, except my mother. She may've been right. The Gentlemen's Club turned out to be a bigger project than I imagined.

Part Three

No Fool Like an Old Fool

1

My employer wasn't in the mood to chew the fat. "I'm a busy man. I've got a well in trouble in Anadarko, a blowout in the Gulf, and a daughter who wants to go to China to save souls." He looked me up and down to see if I might be the reason for his troubles.

"This club's my precious. Make her pretty, don't fuck her up." He gave me a $7500 advance with the promise of a nice bonus if I did better than good.

He turned me over to the club manager, a man as slick as an eel and not at all shy in telling me most of the dancers thought screwing him was in their job description. He confided, "I'm often fucked out."

I wasn't to be. It was okay to paint pictures of the inventory but that was all. Other than for bed companions, I shouldn't want for anything. I was to stay in a well-furnished, well-stocked nearby condo. The boss expected me to deliver. I could take my time as long as I produced.

I should be proud. The Gentlemen's Club was the most expensive, the most exclusive club of its kind in town. A group of professional jocks had voted TGC the best titty bar in the country.

"Yeah," one of the dancers said, "you don't have to give head in a phone booth here." She popped her gum and laughed. I heard later she was fired.

It was good to be back in the flow of commercial work. The job was right up my alley.

Since the dancers were protected by muscular, snake-quick men adept at individual and crowd control, they relaxed around me. One teased that her juices would grow hair anywhere I liked. Would I like a Van Dyke? I declined.

The women had stylish bodies, all right: some natural, most enhanced, but nice. And truth to tell, they had more talent than their nakedness. They not only simulated sex in personal dances—they performed in cabaret numbers.

My work caught something in their eyes, in their teasing lips, in the way they flaunted breasts, in the way they curled and cocked their bodies. Some looked sweet and nice and I captured that tenderness. I caught that in a couple of pictures of nymphs gamboling in exotic mists.

Some had little tenderness left in them. I did my best to make that look sexy for those who liked their sex and business mean and tough.

I painted some especially sexy nudes for The Private Room. My most erotic, however, were saved for the bathrooms. I got a lot of compliments, some even from an art critic or two.

The pictures ran the gamut from conventional big-tit, thick-bush sexiness to bold challenging puckered lips, to quiet eyes and shy smiles, to raucous grins, to the embarrassed coy of one about to disrobe for a lover.

There were tattoos but none gross. There were no tongue studs. There were no facial piercings other than earrings. Most, but not all, wore small diamonds in their navels. Some decorated their pussies.

I didn't have as much of a problem with that as I'd thought I would. What I had trouble with was narrow pubic hair.

The three days became three weeks, and no contact with Vida. I was lost in my work and in something else.

2

The something else was twenty-eight-year-old Carla Luchese, a woman who had gone through three husbands, was working on her fourth, had had more lovers than Vida and been left with two daughters.

Slick saw she was my favorite and tried to warn me her fourth husband was a definite danger. I was too absorbed in the graceful to pay close attention.

Carla gave me the fisheye when I told her she was the best dancer.

"Thanks, but I'm thinking of giving up show business. I'd be better off doing word processing."

She popped her gum. "This kind of work makes me feel cheap." She brushed at a strawberry nipple and patted her belly.

"Some assemblage, huh?" she cracked.

"Not perfect, but every body should look so good."

"Is that your way of telling me if I had an ass, I'd rule the world?"

"You've got a great face," I said. I touched some paint to the canvas and looked at her carefully. "You shouldn't feel cheap. You work hard. You take care of your family."

She smiled and I went on. "This is no dive, this is top of the line. Everybody says so."

She laughed, "I know. But all the same, sometimes when I'm out there rolling around naked, my skin just crawls and crawls. I feel creepy all over." She brushed at herself and ran her hands over her body in a beguiling way, covering her breasts with her right arm and placing her left hand over her pubes like a butterfly. She ducked her head, then peered up at me.

I said, "Great!" and thought, Great, a response just a step ahead of *Shit*. "I mean it."

"You make me feel good. You make me feel proud." She gave me a warming smile I hadn't seen before.

"I'm almost finished," I said.

"I could pose for you all day everyday. How much could you pay?"

"Not as much as you make here."

"At least I wouldn't feel guilty."

"I'm afraid the work wouldn't be steady." I tried to concentrate.

"True. I am sort of protected here. I can choose what kind of shit to take." She popped her gum and her face turned hard.

"Don't lose the pose," I said.

"I worked a place once where you'd swing down the runway, pick out a guy, lay down in front of him and let him have a good look at her, hoping maybe he'd lay a five there. The idea was to make her wink. A real high-class joint."

"Sounds like my kind of place," I said.

"Not exactly my kind either." She took a deep breath or two. "I read somewhere taking deep breaths is good for you." She took another. She saw me watching her breasts rise and fall. "I don't mean to embarrass you."

"I'm not embarrassed," I said. But I was.

"I had this one old faithful who'd come in, tie a napkin around his neck and beg me to let him, well, you know. I never did. I drove him right up the wall." She looked at what I'd painted. "He always behaved. He always gave me more money than the others. He was a funny old guy. He begged to kiss my nipples."

I kept my eyes on the painting.

"Good money some nights, but so fucking humiliating, so fucking degrading, such a fucking travesty, really." She was always tying words together like that. You expected the *fucking*, but not *humiliating* or *degrading* or *travesty*.

She was startling and shocking. Plus she was funny. And mean too, according to some of the girls. I didn't see it.

"Does that make you hot? You're so red in the face."

"I'm sorry you had to work there. It makes me angry."

"That's sweet." (The sweet was a surprise too.) She smiled. "You know, I never fuck or make love for money."

I must've looked skeptical.

"I mean for money alone. If I liked someone and we made love and he gave me money, that'd be all right. But not for money alone."

"For love alone?" There was nothing more I could do for the picture.

"I used to but not now. Once I did it because this guy did my taxes and got me some money back." She stretched and twisted and looked cute. "That was old-time gratitude more than money. I liked the guy but I didn't love him. What about you? Why do you do it? Do you do it because you can't help it? Men have told me that." She looked me up and down. "You're a nice guy. Do you do it for love alone?"

"My time's behind me."

"I don't believe that." She cupped my chin and smiled. "You're sweet." She kissed me on the lips. The kiss started out a light touch but lingered and changed.

"That was nice," she said. "I have to be going. My kids."

"Yes." I thought, No fool like an old fool, then put the thought away.

"You know what that kiss tells me?"

"No."

"It tells me you're not a harmless old man. Your time's not behind you. That's just a ploy. You've got more than your share left." She dressed in a way that was sexier than when she stripped.

"All this may look tacky but dancing is an art. I'm an artist. The world may not think so, but I am. I'm not just a piece of meat on display. You don't think of me as a piece of meat, do you?"

"No, I don't."

"Got to run. My babies." She pecked me on the cheek.

"I have a lot of hope," she said. "I believe in hope, don't you?"

"I saw a bumper sticker the other day—'I feel so much better now that I've given up hope.' —But if hope's good enough for you, it's good enough for me."

She laughed and left.

I didn't care if she was teasing and having some fun at my expense, or even being a touch cruel. I didn't mind at all, not at all. I didn't wonder if I was getting in over my head or where this was going. I didn't care if my glands and imagination were working overtime. I didn't ask who was fooling who. I thought, Let it ride, let it go, see what happens. —If you can call that a thought.

3

She looked at me a little ashamed. I smiled what felt like an awkward smile and turned my head.

"How noticeable is it?" she asked.

I pretended not to hear.

"Oh, come on, Wayman, be straight with me. How bad is it?"

"Not too bad."

"But it is noticeable, isn't it? For God's sakes, answer me." She studied her reflection.

"You did a good job with your makeup. A person has to be looking for it."

"Oh, well," she said, fussing with her hair. "Black eyes are black eyes. They go away in time."

"That they do."

"The customers will eat it up." She made faces at herself in the mirror. She squalled like a cat and made her fingers into cat's claws. "What'd you think?"

"They'll be sympathetic," I said.

"Fat chance. They'll think I got what I asked for. Most of 'em'll wish *they'd* smacked me." She smoothed her makeup. "Oh well, nothing for it anyway. Besides, look on the bright side. No broken nose, no busted lip, and no other visible bruises this time." She gave me a killing look. "This isn't the first time he's thumped on me, you know."

I didn't ask why and how often. I felt pity and anger and helpless.

"You ever notice, Wayman, when a girl has a bruise high up on the inside of her thigh, how excited you men get? You ever think of that? You men like to think that's a sign of slumbering passion just waiting to come all over you. You think some great big pleasure caused it, like she begged to be hit and pinched and bitten." She splotched red. "I can tell you right now it didn't happen that way. More than likely, she bumped into a table. You men are such fools."

"I've noticed," I said.

She purred. "Does that excite you? You get off on that?" She almost broke up, but she stayed in character. "Don't you have any finer feelings? Are you nothing but an animal like the rest of the male sex?" She smiled like a cat closing in. "Come on, old man, hit me, pinch me, bite me, tell me the truth." She wrapped her arms around me and kissed me.

"I'm sure you know more about men than I do," I said.

"You think so, huh?" She stepped back and sat on a stool, taking a break from being on the prowl.

"You're a very appealing woman," I said.

"You think so?" Her smile began as a cynical one, but turned warm. Very tricky but nicely done.

"Yes," I said, thinking Vida wouldn't mind. She loved her work. She would be lost in it. She wouldn't care. I'd be the last thing on her mind.

Anyway, chances were she'd never know. Maybe one of her Pennsylvania Dutch Men had showed up. Whatever, she was a distance away and Carla was near.

None of the other girls had her grace and style. Carla had the best legs. She walked any way she wanted, businesslike, teasing, comic, slinky, sexy. She was more than a satchel-assed, tall drink of water. She was alluring.

She didn't have the largest breasts, but hers were hers, womanly, good and natural to the touch. Her nipples were sassy.

She had a neck that made the hairs on the back of yours stand up. A C-section scar ran along her pubic hairline. Her bush was fertile and untrimmed, wild enough to hide lions in. Her hair was a rich dark brown with a touch of natural red.

She had expressive, inquisitive green eyes. As the saying goes, many women would have killed for her cheekbones. Her face was alive and alert, intense, with a depth of emotion and undeveloped intelligence. Everything about her was a struggling independence.

Altogether, an appealing, striking female, a great woman, a woman, I was certain, more than fond of me.

"I've had guys give me the once over, but not like you did just now. What'd you think? Not much to look at or hot stuff?"

"You can tell what I think from the picture," I said.

"Is that so? Well, let me have a look." She rubbed her eye.

"You know you don't have to take that."

"He is my husband."

"That's no reason."

"You don't know how strong he is."

"You could get help."

"Help? You want to help? You want to take him on?"

I felt foolish. "The police might be better equipped."

"He's a cop," she said as if that was the end of that.

"There're other agencies. You could call your minister."

"Like you think I don't go to church." She almost shrieked. "Let me tell you, Mister Wayman, I may not go every Sunday, but I go to church regularly. You ever go?"

"Not for years," I said.

"You can come with me some Sunday," she said.

"Fine. Anytime." I figured it was all so much talk.

"You ever hit a woman?" she asked. "Never mind, I withdraw the question."

"That's okay. I got over it years ago."

"May I ask you a personal question?"

"Shoot."

"Do you like women?" she asked.

"Some," I said, wondering what she was driving at.

"Are you married?"

"No," I said, wondering why the coyness.

"Are you gay?"

I didn't answer right away.

"You don't have to be ashamed if you are," she said. "I just want to know if you sleep with men. Nothing to be touchy about."

"No," I said, a hair pissed off, as she would've put it.

"Good. Do you have any STD's?"

"For Christ's sake, no."

"Great. Sean Kevin has kicked me out of the house and taken the girls. I literally need a place to stay."

"You don't have to put up with that, cop or no cop," I said.

"I know, but answer the question. May I move in with you? For a few days—until I can find another place."

She was a mixture of toughness and helplessness. I didn't know why I said what I said. I suppose I meant it as a joke.

"You could always shoot him, you know."

"Be serious. I'd probably miss and shoot myself. Well, how's about it?"

"Sure, why not? Sounds like fun."

4

The first thing Carla said as she slid into bed was, "If you don't use your energy, Wayman, you'll lose it."

"Do you have any STD's?" I asked.

"No, silly. And I don't do cocaine or crack or ecstasy on a steady basis," she said mischievously. "I have injected heroin into my beautiful body only once and never again. I don't smoke dope very often and will not around here. I do drink alcohol, sometimes to excess, but I don't feel the need of it. —Plus I have dropped acid a hundred and fifty-three times in my life."

I felt like the original callow youth.

"You keep count?" I asked.

"You bet I do."

"Aren't you afraid you'll fry your brains?"

"You think my brains are fried?" She let the sheet fall from her breasts. I wished I'd had her right nipple in my mouth.

"Well, do you?"

"No, I don't," I apologized.

"The secret is in the mics. Don't over mic."

"I see."

"I have access to some really good acid."

"Please, no need to bother on my account."

"Well, okay, but you know a lot of artists say acid is better than good head. It gives them new visions."

"Thanks anyway. I have enough visions to last this lifetime." I wondered if I did.

"Jesus, try to do somebody a favor and they bite your head off. I'm not pushing anything, I'm just trying to be friendly."

"Sorry," I said.

"Oh, Wayman, don't be so testy." She did a little wriggle. "Let's see what shape your energy's in."

It seemed to be in pretty good shape. Not my best, but serviceable. She moaned once or twice. I might have been too heavy. My pride put it down to pleasure.

5

The following weekend Carla was to be gone both Saturday and Sunday. "The girls," was all she said.

So footloose and with nothing but time on my hands I drove to Burro to see Vida. I had never been in a situation like this one: New and unsettling and exciting for an old man.

I wondered what Vida would think of Carla, not that I was going to tell her. It was just that Carla would have interested her. Carla was from a prosperous family with a farm near Bastrop. She ran away from home when she was thirteen, fourteen, fifteen, her age changed each time she told the story—sometimes a hint of incest crept in, but I never asked and she never elaborated.

One thing never changed, she had Temple when she was fifteen because, she said, she was marshmallow fat and took affection any way she could. Finally, neither the school or her mother or her father could handle her. A psychologist said she fucked too much. "The best thing to do is have her institutionalized."

"I hated that word. —So, I hit the road. And here I am, on the rise. As soon as I get shut of Sean Kevin, nothing but smooth sailing."

I crossed into Sage County. I wondered if Ronnie had his spies out.

I didn't go by the home. Instead I visited my father's grave at the Burro Free Cemetery, something I hadn't done in years. I paid the association to keep the weeds out and to put flowers on it now and then. It was obvious the attendants needed speaking to. I made a mental note to get a new headstone the next chance I had.

A young couple was sprucing up a grave. I heard the woman say "Sure is nice she's still dead." I guessed the *she* was his mother. The young man turned sour then saw me and grinned. I had the feeling if I hadn't been there, he would've popped her. Which made me wonder if I should track down Sean Kevin and try to talk sense into him. He needed help, more than Carla. Maybe I was the one to do it.

I suddenly realized the kind of chance I was taking sleeping with another man's wife. I let the realization slide.

I stopped by the Cafe Moroney for a glass of ice tea. Isabel was warm and friendly. Henry was there. He cracked wise about my not having Vida to protect me. Maybe he could serve as a tune up for Sean Kevin. In my sweet childish way, I told him he should do whatever he felt comfortable with. He didn't move.

With no tune up, I went by my place and aired it out. I could've sworn Vida's portraits looked at me like they knew what I was up to. There was nothing to do but face Vida.

I parked in her back driveway and hoped she wouldn't trick me into a confession.

Her back door was open, the screen door unlatched. I scraped my shoes on the steps, coughed a couple of times and banged the door. No response. I went through the same routine. Still no response.

No *Come in, the door's open,* no *Be with you in a minute,* no *Make yourself at home.* No sound. Nothing. I went weak-kneed.

"Knock knock. Company. Yoo-hoo, Vida. Company!"

Still nothing.

I tiptoed. My heart pinched and hurt. I bumped against a kitchen chair and sent it rattling across the room. Nothing.

I eased into the command center living room, where she was lost in concentration, consumed by her computer. She let me stand there like a bump on a log, until my back ached. Finally,

"Wayman, isn't this the most wonderful device? I've fallen in love all over again with my computer." She rose and gave me a godly hug. How different she felt from Carla. How vigorous and strong she was in her own way.

"You hug like a man with a guilty conscience," she said. "You haven't taken up with a sweet young thing in the city, have you?"

"No, of course not." The lie rattled around the room. I wondered if Dorothy had found out about Carla and had snitched on me.

"You look like a man who's been burning the candle at both ends." She studied me carefully.

"I've been working hard," I said.

"What brings you here?" Her directness stung.

"I needed a break, I wanted to see you. I thought we might go out to the lake for a bite to eat." I was more nervous than I thought I'd be.

"Sounds good to me."

We didn't say a word on the way. When we got to the restaurant we sat and looked at the speedboats spawning rooster tails.

"My computer is a godsend. Now, let's see, what do I want, chicken fried steak or catfish?"

"Whatever you say." I was nervous but happy to be with her.

"I'll have the fried catfish with French fries and a bucket of coleslaw and dozens of hushpuppies and all the ice tea I can drink. I hope you have lots of money because I'm starving."

The catfish was fresh and white and nice and succulent. The hush puppies were hot and spicy, the French fries mediocre. Vida drowned her fries in catsup, something I'd never seen her do before. She praised the coleslaw no end, and all in all ate like a horse. She finished with a big bowl of strawberries and thick cream.

We were as full as ticks and our bellies showed it.

"Thanks for remembering," she said.

Remembering? Remembering what? Remembering her?

"I don't feel so bad, seeing you've forgotten," she said.

"I haven't forgotten," I said.

"Don't lie to me, Wayman. You're as transparent as glass."

"I could never lie to you, Vida." That sounded so bad we both laughed.

"All right, since you don't remember, I'll tell you. This is our anniversary. A year gone by in the blink of an eye. Wasn't that a time!"

"It certainly was," I said, thinking it hadn't been a year, but if she wanted it so, fine.

She smiled and we didn't talk until we got back to her place. Then she started trying to tell me what she could do on the computer. She could keep track of things, plan courses, set up projects, run test models to test theories.

Her eyes glistened, her face was alive.

"Esperanza's excited. You know, Wayman . . . ."

I had not come for another lecture, but she had me.

"When you are building something new, it is essential to be thorough and careful. Passion accounts for a lot, but the details do it."

She smiled. She hadn't been so happy and pleased since my show. "Change has to be natural and come from existing seeds and even then you couldn't always control the results. Chaos." She laughed.

I started to ask if Hillman Doe was around, but she was so excited I got lost in her enthusiasm.

"Look!" She showed me graphics and designs and inventories that could've been weapons or loaves of bread. She was happy.

We didn't say much the rest of the day or into the night. She let me stay so we could rock each other in our arms and make love in our fashion.

6

She was working when I got up.

I fixed a breakfast of poached eggs and orange juice, which she gulped down. I did the dishes, then we went out to my place. She worked like a Turk. She was old but not feeble.

I gave her the portrait of her on a fig as an anniversary present.

She said she loved it and would treasure it until eternity came knocking, then laughed. "Silly, it's not our anniversary. Whatever on earth made you think it was? You're so full of baloney it's terrible."

It was nice seeing her in a good mood, even when she asked how I was making out in town. I told her about the girls at the club without saying much about Carla.

"Do you have a favorite?" she asked.

"Vida Singer, but you know that."

"So I do," she said.

"It's true."

"Don't make it worse than it is."

I tried to look her in the eye but couldn't hold it. We drove back to her place in silence.

I thanked her for her help and tried to help her inside but she wouldn't let me.

She said, "When you get over whatever's holding you down there, come on back. There's lots to be done around here."

"I don't have anything to get over." I tried to look serious but broke into a smile.

"At least you have the decency to know you're lying. Goodbye, Wayman. See you, perhaps."

I hugged her. I loved her so. She went in looking a touch bent but independent as ever.

I headed back to Fort Seneca, thinking life was pretty grand after all. Here I was an old man involved with and loving two of the most unusual women a man could imagine; a genius of an old woman near the end and a young woman in full bloom in the struggle of life.

Fucking A—I was living proof a man could love two women at the same time. —Even three. All I needed to be complete was a woman about my age, maybe five, ten years younger, provided I could find the time to fit her in.

7

"**S**urprise!" Carla said and threw her arms around my neck and gave me a big kiss.

Quite a surprise it was. She had moved her two daughters in with us. Temple, scarcely thirteen, already had the look of a woman, while eleven-year-old Cartier thought herself to be of movie-star quality and acted accordingly.

"Cartier?" I raised an eyebrow at Carla.

"I got tired of Tiffany, so I decided to start a new fad. Voila, Cartier."

Cartier looked defiant. I said, "Fine by me."

I offered to move out, but Carla said No, the girls had their sleeping bags, it was only for a few days and they were used to seeing a man and a woman in bed together—they were mature beyond their years.

The three of them made me uneasy, especially the girls in their underwear or less. Not that their young sexuality had a hold over me, but the last thing I needed was a misguided, misinformed, outraged social worker coming down on me.

I admired their youth without envy. What I didn't admire was the way the three of them feasted off their sudden squall-like quarrels that rocked the place without clearing the air.

The few days grew into more. I became fond of the girls although I knew nothing about raising them. No matter what I did, they weren't shy in telling me Sean Kevin would have done it better. I expected the kindly, avenging Sean Kevin to show any day.

I felt like a guilty old innocent who had succumbed to too much temptation. Carla said I shouldn't concern myself. She became absorbed in a self-help TV college credit course, *Ethics and the*

Good Society, which came on on Saturday mornings. Each Saturday morning she sent the girls out so she could study. She wouldn't let me go along. She said she needed me.

"Tell me, Wayman," Carla started in her formal way when she had a paper to write, "do you think The Gentleman's Club would exist in a good society? Would the good society be so good as to have no room for me and The Gentleman's Club? What do you think?"

"I rarely think about the Good Society," I said, feeling a Vida tinge in my chest.

"That's a shame. You should. You really should."

"I suppose so. The Good Society? You haven't run into someone named Vida, have you?"

"No, who's she?"

"A woman who teaches and preaches about societies and the world. Used to make blue movies, so the story goes. I thought you might have heard of her."

"Where do you know her from?" She sounded suspicious and serious.

"I read about her somewhere," I said. "She may be dead now. She was a crackpot of sorts." I didn't feel like the most noble son of a bitch in the world right then.

"Too bad about her, but answer the question, please: Would the Good Society permit me and The Gentleman's Club to exist?" Without giving me a chance to answer, she stormed about like an adolescent. "I have to know, damn it. I have to write this theme and you know how hard it is for me to write a theme. I can't put my thoughts down the way I think them and I don't know why. Sometimes I wish I hadn't started this fucking course."

Her electric mood flashes weren't as charming as they once were. They had a scary edge to them.

"Well now, I don't know much about good or bad societies," I said, drawling the words out, trying to make her laugh, "but I'm sure it wouldn't be a very good society without Carla Luchese."

She beamed. "You know what I like about you, Wayman? I mean really like," her bad mood vanishing. "You never bitch me out. You never do." A loving mood made her soft and warm and shining.

"Let's check your energy," she said playfully.

"The girls," I said. "The girls."

"What about the girls? We aren't news to them. They're not innocents, you know."

How quickly the hard look came. She stripped and walked around the room.

"For Christ's sakes, Wayman, we have our lives to live. At least I have mine to live." Then another change. "I'm only teasing. They won't be back for hours."

That worried me. Where on God's green earth could they be? What could they be doing? I'd never been a real father and felt lost.

"You're sweet, Wayman," her warmth returning, "but not to worry. They'll take care of themselves, they're my children, after all."

She turned so I could see her naked body better. "I'm no fucking saint, but I'm not evil either. I'm good for you." She smiled.

I laid my face against her tender belly. "That's the boy," she said.

8

Saturday morning Carla said she was skipping her TV class, the subject was all bullshit anyway, and she was due at the club to run through some new routines.

The girls went off on their own arguing. I gave them some money and they thanked me in a bitchy sort of way. Cartier was upset because Temple could menstruate and have babies and she couldn't. A debate I had no way of dealing with.

I waited for them to return until I couldn't stand it any more. I called Carla who said relax, that if I couldn't relax, I should call the police or better still Sean Kevin. 'If you're all that hot and bothered, go look for them yourself.'

Come hell or high water, I was to leave her alone. She was busy, the dances were fucking intricate, I should be more considerate. The girls could take care of themselves! The phone came down hard.

I knew it wouldn't do any good to call the police, and there was no reason to have a run-in with Sean Kevin right now. I was old enough to know that the better part of valor is discretion.

I drove the main highways leading out of town. No sign of them.

I gave the amusement park a lick-and-a-promise search. Nowhere to be seen.

I called a couple of movie theaters. No luck. Useless.

I hit the malls with their enormous attraction for girls that age with their shops, department stores, boutiques, food courts, electronic games, and boys. Yes, boys, young men, and men.

My heart jumped into my throat when I saw them, except the them turned out not to be my them. I wondered where my tykes could be. Tough little nuts. Poor things.

I searched mall parking lots. Girls disappeared from them almost daily. All you had to do was pick up a paper or listen to the radio or watch TV and there was a story of a girl abducted from a mall parking lot and found dead in a ditch or in the river, left in a park or on a back road.

I came up on some boys trying to break into a car. They scattered like quail, thank God.

I gave up on the malls and eased through the section of town where folks live who'll never have to worry where their next diamond is coming from. There were enough colonials, modern castles, and in-city estates to trick you into believing God's in His Heaven and all's right with the world. No Temple. No Cartier. Only looks of what are you and your truck doing here. Make your delivery and leave.

I moved through an area of ranch houses on low rolling slopes, with the same result.

I went through the zoo. No sign of my little monkeys.

I could no longer run from thoughts of marijuana, cocaine, smack, heroin, PCP, LSD, Ecstasy, or was it XTC, and angel dust. The promise of escape, peace and joy and visions, might just be what the girls were after. I blamed Carla, their fathers, Sean Kevin, their self-centeredness, their self-destructiveness. I blamed their grandparents and finally me for their isolation.

The section where dealers and prostitutes ruled like feudal kings and queens had once been a fine middle-class community but not now.

One street was flooded with women in sexy getups. A car eased by, made a circle, came back and stopped close to a woman who looked like a comic book version of an African Princess from a Tarzan movie. A large white hand shot out and began massaging a big black breast. Quick as a wink, that Princess jerked the man from his car. She slammed him against the hood while she cuffed him. I had wandered into a police sting.

A motorcycle cop pulled up next to me.

"Want something, Pop?"

"No."

"Then get the hell out of the way. Quick!"

I moved as far to the side as fast as I could without winding up in the ditch. A convoy of screaming motorcycles and patrol cars cleared the way for a black olive motor vehicle twice the size of any tank I'd ever seen, carrying a mean looking battering ram.

Without hesitation the ram smashed a small frame house to bits, then did the same to a brick house and moved on.

"I thought I told you to get out of here," the cop said.

"On my way," I said, grateful the girls weren't there.

I didn't know where to look next, so I drove out to Dorothy's, hoping I might see the girls on the way.

No sign of the girls.

Dorothy kissed me and asked about Vida and what brought me to town.

"Anything wrong?"

I didn't answer.

"Smile if you've been getting any different pussy."

I couldn't help smiling. I caved in. I told her about the girls and Carla. She said she wouldn't tell Vida but I should go home before I found myself in some very deep shit. I thanked her for being a jewel and left.

It was now dark. I had one more place to try, the home for street people under the viaduct.

No sooner had I parked than more than a panhandler put the arm on me. A woman with a face like a white mask sat on a torn suitcase and yelled, "No house! No home! No house, no home!"

A peculiar community with neat rows of dark quilt and newspaper pallets spread out in nearby parking lots. Some people were already lying down, some talking, some drinking, some counting their day's take. A few sorted through gift packages left by various groups. Some curled up like dark pine knots on their pallets.

Thank God, the girls weren't there. I didn't know where to look next. I was worn to a frazzle. I went back to my condo. The only thing left was to call the police.

The lights were on. Loud music. Someone was spreading his culture about. I figured Sean Kevin was waiting to whip my ass. I heard deep-throated laughter. The son of a bitch and Carla were making love, not giving one thought to the girls.

I hit the door hard, eager to spill frustration and anger and righteousness all over them.

But it wasn't Sean Kevin and Carla. It was Carla and Temple and Cartier having a big time, singing and listening to rock-and-roll hymns.

"We were just about to go out looking for you. Where've you been? We were worried."

The girls gave me big hugs. I was too happy to scold.

"Carla's got some news!" Temple said with a twist to her mouth.

"I'll say I have. I've quit The Gentleman's Club and put myself in the hands of the Lord. How about that!"

I looked at her carefully. She had a new, unnatural, freshly-washed look about her. I wondered if I was to be the hand of the Lord.

"The first thing tomorrow. The four of us are going to church."

"I'll be damned," I said.

"Not if you give yourself to the Lord," Carla said. "You showed me the way, Wayman. I'll always be grateful." She looked completely relieved.

"Yes, thank you." I had no idea what she meant. I was only glad my wise little devils were home.

After the girls giggled themselves to sleep, I asked Carla why she'd quit. She said again it was my doing. I didn't follow.

"What're you going to do?"

"The Lord will provide." She took her time and looked me over.

"You know Wayman, until now I never thought religion had anything in it for me. Can you understand that?"

I said yes I could and did.

"I was convinced everything I'd ever thought and done was right until I met you. Everything. You and that cute young minister on TV, both of you, helped me. I'm telling you, Wayman, the Lord is at work in my life. I see an overall purpose where I saw none." She took a breath and looked me in the eye.

"Do you have any idea at all how transformed I am?"

Another of her unexpected words, I was almost too tired to appreciate it.

"Never mind. I can see you're weary. Go to bed. I'll sleep on the floor. I was only wondering if you're capable of understanding me."

I smiled and said without wishing to start a fight, "I think I'm capable."

"That makes me happy. Pleasant dreams."

I went to bed, figuring this too shall pass. I expected to lay there and twitch, but I didn't. If Carla and the girls were happy, so was I. I slept like a baby.

9

The next morning I woke up to the smell of frying sausage. I lay there in my underwear wishing Carla and the girls would disappear so I could get up without embarrassing myself. I did not want to walk around in front of the girls in nothing but my underwear. I was not like Carla, who could traipse around in her see-through panties or even buck-naked in front of the girls. I'd spoken to her about it more than once. Each time she'd assured me I was a foolish old man who understood little of the modern world. I allowed as how she could be right.

The three were dressed and looked like birds perched on a fence, waiting for me to get up.

"Breakfast," Cartier commanded.

"Rise and shine, Lazy Bones. A new day dawns." Carla tugged at my sheet.

Temple laughed.

I thought, What the hell and got up.

"What shall I wear?"

"As far as the Lord's concerned, you can come as you are," Carla said.

"Must be casual day at the Lord's house," I said.

The girls laughed. I felt better.

Carla cut her eyes and said seriously, "No man's raiment is an embarrassment unto the Lord."

I thought, Shit! I found my pink shirt, an old blue knit tie, a pair of presentable charcoal-gray trousers and my frayed-around-the-edges blue blazer. Mr. Spiffy.

The girls looked splendid in their blue and yellow dresses. Each carried a white Bible, which had appeared out of nowhere.

Carla looked blessed in her blue dress and small hat with a veil. I couldn't remember the last time I'd seen a woman her age, or my age, or any age, in a veil.

"Ready to receive your blessings?"

"Ready as I'll ever be," I said softly. The last thing I wanted to do was tick her off.

"Hurry up," Cartier said.

Temple muttered, "This better not be a waste of time."

"Wipe that look off your face before I wipe it off for you," Carla snapped.

Cartier swallowed a giggle. Temple flared.

But before she and Carla could get into it, I said, "Look at me. I can't get any prettier. It must be time to leave."

It didn't make the three all that happy, but things got a little better. We left to frowns but not a fight.

10

The church looked like it belonged on the frontier, surrounded by a different kind of hostiles. It was a small white clapboard structure topped by a just-right steeple which Cartier called a sticker. It was the kind of church that made you want to go inside. It suggested a certain kind of old-fashioned comfort.

Temple took one look and whispered, "The Church of the Whizz Bang."

Carla pinched her so hard I thought the girl was going to scream, but she bit her lip and saved her anger.

The pews were long and yellow. I settled in and felt right at home. The girls liked the rock-and-roll beat of the hymns. "Holy, Holy, Holy" was more my style.

The minister was young and thin and cute and a touch arrogant but appealing as he offered communion. If we wanted to believe or did believe that the crackers and grape juice became the actual flesh and blood of Jesus, that was marvelous and fine with him. If we preferred to think of the crackers and juice as symbols, that was A-Okay too. Any other beliefs and interpretations were welcomed as well. The important thing was communion.

The girls helped themselves. Carla partook in silence. I abstained despite an unexpected urge for communion. I wished Vida were with us.

The girls put their offerings in the basket cheerfully enough. I slipped mine in as casually as I could. I didn't watch Carla because I didn't want to know how much she put in or took out.

The young preacher looked content and happy and serious, at home in the pulpit.

His sermon, "In Praise of Lowlifes," went something like this:

"One of my hobbies is reading detective stories. Not highbrow but good old-fashioned pulp, a distinguished order of trash, at best. I hope that doesn't shock you."

Titters.

"Some of the characters are adulterers, murderers, pedophiles, thieves, dealers, slavers, rapists, incestuous beings, who hide behind the facades of success and goodness, but many are out in the open, drunks and prostitutes, bums and whores. Lowlifes supreme."

More titters.

"Recently, a famous critic jumped all over the author of such creations. —'Why write about such as these? Who can be interested in such lowlifes?'

"I'll tell you who's interested in these people: the Creator and the Lord, that's who! Is that an answer for you?"

Amens.

"Most of us are like the critic. We don't want to be around bums and drunks, down-and-outers. Men and women who have the dirt of ages ground into their faces—people who stink to high heaven—bums, dope addicts, child molesters, thieves, pimps— Beat up, beat down, worn-out old whores and whoremongers— God-forsaken queers. —If such a thing were to come along and sit next to us, not one of us would stay seated there. We'd change seats in a flash, and feel good about it.

"But the Lord wouldn't. He, or She, if you prefer, might want to bathe them, but the Spirit wouldn't move away. —The Spirit would engulf them.

"What the critic missed, what you and I miss, is not only compassion, but that some lowlifes like you and me make the world turn. Without us, them, nothing would get done.

"So let's not condemn too quickly, let's do more than scorn, lest we be condemning ourselves.

"So what do we do? We can't escape.

"My friends, two things abound in this world, crap and God's Grace. The trouble is most of the time we seem to take God's Grace for crap.

"Wouldn't it be something if the Lord used Lowlifes to bring the Kingdom of God to our world?"

I had some trouble following his train of thought, but after the devastation of yesterday, I wondered if my being there were the result of a higher will. I needed Vida to tell me I was giving a couple of unrelated events more significance than they deserved.

There was no doubt the man was effective. When he issued the Invitation to come forward and join with them, it was all I could do to hold back.

"That was some service, Carla. Thanks for making me come."

"You may've liked it, Wayman, but I didn't. The man had no business preaching like that in front of children. He doesn't know shit about lowlifes."

Shit is only a little word, but more than a few eyebrows went up; more than one hard angry look came Carla's way.

The preacher took no offense. He thanked her for coming. She shook his hand and thanked him in return. I thought her eyes said he just might be her next.

"An interesting service," I said.

"Thank you. Fine looking girls. Your granddaughters?"

"No."

"Well, a man can't have everything." He smiled. "I didn't see your retrospective until a week after it opened. I enjoyed it. Like your shirt and tie. Love your truck." He was a funny young man.

But Carla's father wasn't a funny old man. He was heavy and somber and serious as he sat in his pickup waiting for us outside the condo.

11

The man jumped down from the cab as soon as he saw us. He looked as strong as an orangutan.

I was a complete surprise to him. My smile and the fact I was a good ten years older made him turn away. When he did look me in the eye again, it was no longer with iron but grief.

"Carl Holtzer," he said extending his hand.

"Wayman Scott." His hand was not quite as big as Traber's, but it showed a lifetime of hard work.

"I've come for the girls," he said.

Carla looked at her father with cold passion, a long-term, get-even threat.

The girls looked at their grandfather, Carla, then me. "You all want to go?" I asked. They were confused.

"It's all right," I said.

"Your grandmother has some nice things for you," he said.

Cartier looked like the old woman better have. Carla didn't say a thing.

"I'll come as long as I can ride in the back," Temple said.

The man didn't like that, but he nodded.

Cartier said, "I want to ride up front so I can snuggle up to Paw-Paw."

I invited him in while the girls packed. He said he preferred the outside. I offered him a beer. He said no. A coke? No. He accepted a glass of water.

The girls were packed in no time. Carla refused their hugs, but I didn't.

The girls got aboard.

The man and I shook hands again. For an uneasy moment I thought he was going to break my hand.

"Thank you for taking care of the girls." The man looked ready to cry.

"They're fine girls. A real treat."

"I suppose you mean well."

"Sometimes."

"Come home soon, girl."

"Never, Papa. I said never and I meant never." I had heard the harshness in her voice before but hadn't taken the trouble to believe it.

"Your mother and I'll take good care of them." He paused. "We miss you, darlin'."

Carla's face went even tighter.

I waved as they drove off. I looked at Carla and supposed it would do no good to shake her until she rattled.

"I'll be back later." She got in her red flame-thrower and dug out for all she was worth.

"Fine, I've got a few things to attend to anyway," I said after her.

I wondered what Vida would think.

Two pictures came to my mind. One was the look of fear and joy on Temple's face as her grandfather's pickup sped away with her in the back with the suitcases. The other was the mural on the convenience store-icehouse near the leveled crack houses, the blue ocean lapping against a white beach while a bare-breasted, sensual black woman stood waist deep and watched brown pelicans overhead. I wondered who painted it and why there.

I went to work. It must've been one-thirty, two o'clock before I climbed into bed. No Carla. Maybe in her quick way she'd decided to pack it in. A not completely unpleasant thought, except I would miss her. I didn't bother to trouble with why she was what she was and what she did.

Maybe it was time to get out of town, to let my itchy feet, the higher powers or the roll of the dice have their way.

I went to sleep with a funny sort of trembling running through me.

"Sorry to wake you and sorry about this afternoon," Carla said lying naked on me. I hadn't heard her come in or felt her climb up on me.

She did a sissy pushup resting on her arms and letting her breasts tease against my chest, a very pleasant feeling.

"I never said I was a saint, but I'm no ogre either."

I wondered what she was driving at, but I was too tired to ask. I said, "People get out of whack and it takes time to get back in line." I wanted to go back to sleep.

"You're so full of wisdom." She stretched. We were toe to toe and mouth to mouth. She felt good. She pulled my underwear off.

"I just want to feel you against me."

She seemed to have put her newly found beliefs on hold for a while. We went to sleep like babes.

12

Some say the older you are the more fitful your sleep, but I was lost in the sleep of an ancient innocent when the door burst open like a shot. My first thought was Sean Kevin had come to kill us. But it wasn't the wayward husband. It was two overgrown hulks with big pistols in their big hands.

"Trust we didn't wake you all," the older one cracked.

"Up and at 'em. Time to get up," the younger of the two thought he was funny. "Rise and shine."

Carla sat up, but flopped back down. She looked more exasperated than terrified.

I said, "What the hell's going on? Who the hell are you and what're you doing in my home?"

"Get up, old man." The younger looked like he wanted nothing better than to lose his patience.

"Hold your horses. We're unarmed."

The younger stuck the pistol right at my nose. "Please, sir, get out of bed. Slowly."

"The trouble is it's hard to move, even slowly, with a pistol in my face." I felt surprisingly calm. "I said we were unarmed."

"Then get up like the man asks, so we can see," the older said.

"I'm not moving until I know who you bastards are," Carla said. I admired her courage but wished she'd taken a different tack.

"We're your friendly neighborhood police. Friends of Sean Kevin. Now will you get up?"

I admired his sarcasm.

"Hokay." I made a joke. No one laughed. I got up and stood there naked. "See. Unarmed." I did a full three-sixty then reached for my pants.

"Not so fast, Pop. Your turn, Ms. Luchese."

"You bastards," Carla slid out of bed slowly. She showed a lot more defiance than I did. She made no attempt to hide her nakedness. "Look all you want."

Finally, I took my hands away from what she liked to call my organs.

"Aren't you all a pretty sight?" the older one said.

"That's some post-hole digger you got there. You give it to her pretty good?" The younger man was a sorry son of a bitch.

"I don't need that," I said. "Identification?"

"And a warrant," Carla added.

"I'm surprised you didn't ask sooner."

"I did," Carla said.

The two didn't like that. But the older one showed his ID and the younger followed suit. Their badges were big and bright.

"Thank you."

"Here's your warrant, Mister Wayman Ezekiel Scott. That is your name?"

I was still trying to figure out what and why.

"I said, 'That is your name?'" He wasn't happy.

"Yes. Goddamn it, yes!" I could not believe what was going on.

"Be cool, old man, be cool." Young one was more than a pain in the ass. He was mean.

"And here's an arrest warrant for one Ms. Carla Ursula Luchese. You, my dear, are the said Carla Ursula Luchese?"

"Yes." A mean yes. I had the feeling Carla would have killed them without any guilt.

"Leave her alone. She's unarmed," I said.

"We don't know that. You never know what a body search will turn up." The younger one loved his power. He grinned and took a step toward Carla.

I said, "No need for that."

She said, "Cocksucker!"

I wished she'd been a little softer. I said quietly, "What's the problem?"

The older one said, "The problem is the murder of one Sean Kevin Luchese."

"As if you didn't know," the younger chimed.

My anus tightened in a new way. I looked at Carla. She shrugged like so what.

"Let's go."

"Mind if I get dressed?"

"You look pretty good the way you are."

"Fuck you," Carla said.

The way he tightened I thought we were in for it. The older one grinned and threw her a dress. He threw me my trousers and a shirt. That was all. No underwear for either of us, and no shoes.

They read us our rights and handcuffed us. I had never had my rights read to me. The experience did not seem a new one to Carla.

Out of the blue came, "The truth is Wayman put me up to it. It was his idea." She took a breath, "I'm serious. I mean it."

I had the feeling the two had thought I was innocent until then. I looked from the officers to Carla.

She said, "Sorry, I was lonely."

I said, "I understand," not sure that I did.

13

I kept thinking, the shame of it all. Forgetting there's nothing more dangerous than a damsel in distress wasn't the shame of it all. Neither was being handcuffed, accused of murder and hustled about none too gently or being gawked at by the neighbors.

Neither were the TV cameras, the commentators and the questions that came at me like a flood:

"Did you do it for kicks? Because you loved her? Because you loved him?

"You ever stop to think she's young enough to be your granddaughter?

"Do you really love her?

"Did you eat before or after? Did you have sex before or after? How many times? What was it like?

"Were you drunk? Were you high? Was it a dope high or a sugar high?

"What'd you feel as you pulled the trigger? Was it a thrill? Did you get a buzz out of it?

"What about it, old man? You think because you're an artist, you're above the law?

"You a kook, a wacko, a sicko, a cultist?

"You have a vision? Is that it? Voices tell you to kill him?

"What's it like to screw a man's wife then take his life? What's it like to take a man's life then screw his wife? Any remorse?

"What are your feelings at this very moment? Come on, spill your guts, you may save your life.

"Did you do it for her? Or deep down did you do it for yourself? For the thrill? Would you do it again?

"I guess we know the answer to that."

I looked at myself and my haphazard splendor. The farce was in full swing.

The shame of it all wasn't being incarcerated in the notorious Fort Seneca jail, or being booked and searched and processed and hearing steel slam against steel, or testing the thickness of the bars or touching the walls or my inability to use the cold commode; the shame of it all was not being the center of a serious farce, the shame of it all was having to call Vida and ask for help.

Lorrain took my call and said Vida couldn't come to the phone. My call wasn't a surprise, I was quite the celebrity in Burro, another in a long line of Sage County outlaws. People took a cue from my mother and called me Mister Big Shot. Get it, Big Shot. Anyway, I couldn't speak to Vida because she was already on her way to save my worthless hide.

Thank God, the woman hadn't washed her hands of me. My heart settled down.

Vida hit the jail in a swirl. "This is one bad time."

"It's better now you're here."

"This is the worse, if not the worst."

"I agree. I can't tell you how grateful I am."

She put her hands on her hips. "I'm not talking about you. I'm talking about me."

She unloaded. "Do you have any idea what I had to give up to come here?"

Shades of my mother.

"There's no telling how far I'll fall behind. Do you know what that means? Do you care?"

She stared me down. She paced like an angry horse.

"My working days grow shorter as I grow older. Time runs out faster every day. Forces are at work. Time is critical."

I wanted to tell her *Go on back*. But I needed her.

"And to have to come to Fort Seneca to attend to an idiot is not my idea of the best way to get things done, despite its humorous aspects." She smiled.

Seeing the smile, I went on the attack. "Goddamn it, I'm under arrest for murder. I'm in deep trouble. Do you care? Goddamn it, do you?"

She put her arms around me. "If I didn't, I wouldn't have brought an attorney."

I was so surprised I almost said, "Bullshit!"

Thank God, I didn't. And thank God, she'd brought the attorney. He got me released on my own recognizance (a minor miracle in view of the public howl). All I had to do was stay in Fort Seneca through the trial.

14

The romance with Vida's friend didn't last. Old Joe may have been an experienced and proficient criminal attorney, but he was also a leather-necked old fart who kept touching Vida. I took her aside and asked where'd she been keeping Old Joe.

She said, "Don't be more of a damned fool than you already are."

"There are complications," Joe said with a funny smile. "The young woman swears you pleaded with her on a daily basis to get rid of Sean Kevin, her beloved, that you forced her to learn how to shoot."

"Plus the Gestapo claims to have found the murder weapon in your truck," Vida said.

Joe was nothing if not mealy mouthed. "Vida, the police are not the Gestapo. They do the best with what they have," Joe said.

"Speaking of which," Vida said, "some high-grade LSD was found in the freezer. Then there's her diary, which makes for interesting reading."

"I swear I don't know a goddamn thing about any of it."

"Wayman, you poor soul. You may win the lethal needle for being an idiot and nothing else."

"We'll see about that," Old Joe said.

At first I thought he meant no way he'd let that happen, but I decided the bastard would let things slide while pretending to defend me.

"You're fired. I want my daughter."

He said, "You poor dumb bastard."

"I may be, but you're fired."

"Okay, he's fired," Vida said, which didn't make Old Joe very happy.

"I'm innocent. He damn well knows it but he doesn't act like it," I said.

"You're innocent and he's fired. Let's get on with it. I'll send for your daughter." It felt good having Vida in charge.

He said to Vida, "I'll stay in case you need me."

He looked at me and said, "You poor dumb bastard."

15

I had to find a place to stay. My oilman benefactor kicked me out. I asked Dorothy if I could use her little room. She was reluctant but after I whined and begged and promised to behave she said a reluctant Yes.

I told Vida I loved her and could never repay her. She said I know that. I told her I was sorry for what had happened, that I'd learned my lesson. She had to know I loved her. She said, "Yeah, sure."

She softened. "I feel the same way, but let's not go gaga. We both have our work and no telling who or what could come along. You might have to go to jail."

I thanked her for that and asked her to stay the night. She said yes but she had to leave first thing in the morning.

I didn't say a word about old Joe and she didn't say a word about Carla.

I felt much better in the morning.

16

My daughter showed up with a bemused look and said she'd defend me provided I kept my nose clean and we didn't get too chummy, which I didn't see how we could in view of the fee she was charging. Although she wasn't my flesh and blood daughter, she was mine in spirit and had grown into her own person.

I was fair game for the media. Every time a body was found, a collective finger was pointed at me. I should be locked up and the key thrown away.

Not only was I clean. I was squeaky clean. I led an exemplary life. I finished the watercolor of Temple and the acrylic of the icehouse. Dorothy said they were minor masterpieces and in my echelon minor masterpieces were not to be sneezed at.

I became a sign painter for the school. The school had gone merrily on its way with no official name. Most people called it the "Miss Vida Mad Betty Academy." Scoffers called it "The Folly."

The boy came up with the idea that we were all in process, so I painted a bunch of signs IN PROCESS.

I painted others:

AN UNNAMED PROCESS (that scared a lot of folks)

SO WHAT IF WE'RE USELESS, WELCOME ANYWAY (so did that)

There was a great deal of talk about culture in the air, so Vida came up with:

WE ARE YOGURT

then:

WE ARE SALES

WE ARE COMMERCIAL

WE ARE IN PROCESS IN PROGRESS. WE ARE
PROGRESS IN PROCESS
NON PROFIT NON PROPHET NOT FOR YOU. —We
ran that once. I wasn't sure what that meant, but Vida liked it.

I was beginning to think the authorities had forgotten all
about me. Then my daughter appeared with her court face on. The
next day I was in court and scared to death.

17

The judge was an attractive woman on the plump side and no more than thirty-eight. It took a while to get used to hearing people call her "Your Honor." She had a strange smile, a sexy hairdo, and a reputation for delighting in harsh sentences. She believed deeply in the death penalty. I sweated bullets every time I saw her.

The courtroom was packed. Vida and Dorothy came and so did Esperanza and Hillman Doe. He was wanted all over the country for robbing banks and killing, among other things; yet there he sat unafraid in broad daylight for all to see. Esperanza hung on him. I figured the school was on a different track. Vida looked changed.

I couldn't worry too much about her problems, I had my own.

18

I asked my daughter if I had a snowball's chance in Hell. She said, "Barely."

Carl had hired a slick lawyer from Houston for Carla and the prosecutor was a mighty mite of a woman, thirty-one, thirty-two, with no flies on her. She wanted to purify society and the first step was to rid the world of my ass. The judge beamed.

I had trouble keeping up. The trial was a swirl. I didn't recognize the portrait drawn of me in court. Some of the externals were familiar, but not the internals.

I was pictured as a coward, a ne'er-do-well, a hustler, a con man, a charlatan, a seducer of women six times married, a killer, a bigamist.

The prosecution made a big deal out of that. My daughter countered that was only an example of misguided love, a love that caused no harm and gave a child a name.

The prosecution claimed I deliberately abandoned my children, which hurt but which I couldn't deny completely. Somehow my daughter got it in that she never felt abandoned.

I was a contemptible man who ignored and refused to help his mother, a man, who if given the chance, would dance on the grave of the woman who bore him. It didn't seem fair to try me for something that hadn't happened.

I was a beguiler, a sly pied-piper who led an innocent from her loving husband, from her safe haven of bed and board to my licentious bed. Such selfishness. A tempter with dope.

What magic words dope, cocaine, crack are. The jurors' eyes said, "Get on with the execution."

My daughter reminded them that I was not being tried for imaginary crimes or the crimes of others.

But the prosecution, and Carla's attorney, said Wayman Ezekiel Scott is a man who has no shame in exposing himself, a man who has danced naked in the streets, a man who lured those innocent babes Temple and Cartier to his den where he exposed himself to their young eyes many times.

I was an exhibitionist, a *poseur*, a posturer, a man capable of anything, a man with no conscience who had burned Sage County's archives.

"Come on, it's not like we burned the library at Alexandria," Vida said.

"No more outbursts, Miss Singer," the judge said. I began to think Vida's fame might not be an asset.

Most importantly, I was the man behind the trigger, a man to whom death was certainly no stranger—one who had once shot down three men in cold blood without blinking an eye.

My daughter had a fit. He was protecting his country, a soldier doing his duty, not killing the Trinity.

The prosecution brushed that off and hammered away. This man (me?) was the man behind the gun. This man, just as surely as if he had fired the pistol, triggered the murder of Sean Kevin Luchese, husband, father, provider, a decent young man struck down before his time by a master at feathering his own nest, at satisfying his own greed and lust, a genius at plundering and hypnotizing one Carla Ursula Luchese, poor soul, lost mother.

My balls were so cold they burned.

As if that weren't enough, I was called a revolutionary ready to overthrow our world in the guise of forming a perfect society. —Who could believe that?

"Better," said Vida. "Better comes first, then perfect."

"Ms. Singer, please," the judge said.

The prosecutor glowed. "It is from such nuts that the oaks of sedition grow."

The woman swung around and pointed at me.

"This man, Wayman Ezekiel Scott, is a challenge to the peace and dignity of our citizens, our children, our way of life."

She then looked Hillman Doe in the eye, letting Mister Guilty as Sin sit there free while she tried to nail me to the cross. I got the feeling the woman wanted me dead because she didn't like my looks. She assured the jury that my death would make this a better world, immediately. She didn't mean that. She just wanted to be rid of my ass.

Where the prosecutor was hard, my daughter was soft and smooth. Wayman Ezekiel Scott was not the beguiler, but the beguiled, the seduced not the seducer, a lost innocent; an at-times dotty old man with a strange past, but a man of conscience, a war hero, a lover of his country, for what other reason would he try to make it a better place?

"We all know, there's no fool like an old fool, unless it's a loving old fool. And that's what Wayman Scott is. A loving fool trying to make his way in a world too quick for him. —Deep down, each of us knows what that is like."

The jury looked at me a touch more kindly, but then the prosecutor went full bore.

"This man is a cowardly agent of destruction." The woman had mean blue eyes and a smile that erased her lips. She had a voice that roared and cracked and whispered the unthinkable.

"Punish this killer. Extinguish the monster in him."

Not one word for probation, compassion, rehabilitation. The jury looked me over one more time before leaving to see if I was to live or die.

I felt like a piece of chewed string. I thought of moon-faced cattle and sledgehammers.

The jury took their time. A betting man would have put down cash money it was a lead-pipe cinch I'd be found guilty.

The judge lolled around in her robe and was on the phone a lot. More than the trial was going on.

I tried to muster some hate against Carla but couldn't. She was still a fascinating woman in distress who now and then gave me a wave and a wink and looked at me with misty eyes.

My mother wrote:

Dear Son,
   I hear you're having the time of your wasted life, that at long last you are to receive your just desserts.
Your loving but long forgotten,
   Mother.

Oh, well. —Two days went by before the jury announced that they had reached a verdict.

I felt like I'd been sprinkled with porcupine needles. The tips of my fingers were numb. My lips were dry and paralyzed. My heart was frozen. It took my everything to stand and face them. And when I did, I expected the strains of a funeral organ.

What I heard wasn't funeral music but "Not Guilty." I wasn't going to ride on that gurney and have poison poured into my veins.

The prosecutor went white as a sheet. The judge's gasp was heard throughout the courtroom. The jury stood and was polled. Each juror confirmed that *Not Guilty,* was his/her verdict, arrived at independently without force or coercion.

   I didn't give a damn how it was arrived at—it was free for me.

Old Joe looked disappointed, but not Vida or my daughter or Carla. Somehow Carla's attorney, with my daughter's help, got it into the jury's mind that Carla Ursula Luchese killed Sean Kevin Luchese in self-defense. I had nothing to do with it. Sean Kevin begged to be killed and Carla obliged him.

My daughter and the prosecutor and the judge hugged each other like long-lost sisters. They gave each other pointers like it was some game.

The judge sought Vida out and told her she'd long admired Miss Vida.

Neither the judge or the prosecutor said anything to me. I sure didn't say anything to them.

Hillman Doe came up, shook my hand said, "Good show," looked around with a smile, whispered to Esperanza, then melted away.

Esperanza hugged and kissed me and told me I was a good

man. Dorothy kissed me and gave my peter a playful tug. "Behave yourself, you old goat."

Old Joe went up to Vida and said something about justice working in mysterious ways and kissed her. I punched the peckerwood in the nose. He bled like a stuck hog. The picture made TV and the front page.

My daughter smiled and said, "We're even now. That is, we will be when you've paid my fee." We shook hands and she went on her way.

But the strangest was Carla. She hugged my neck and kissed me and told me she thought The Lord had had His hand on us throughout the trial, that I should be grateful. She was.

She asked Vida what she thought, and Vida looked at her with a skeptical but warm smile.

"You are an example for unhappy wives. You made love to your husband, put him to sleep, then shot him in self-defense. It will be interesting to see what you've become when you're my age."

Carla gave her a coy smile. The pair hugged. Carla went on her way.

Vida said, "The farce seems to have ended well. Let's go home."

Home? —Home.

Part Four

Home and Gone

1

Burro. The after effects of the trial made me think about my love for Vida and how I felt about my mother.

My mother said I shouldn't get too cocky merely because I'd gotten away with murder. That didn't matter. During the trial I'd promised myself that no matter what the verdict, I'd tell my mother I loved her. Not an easy thing to do.

She looked right at me. "I don't believe you." Then she said, "I knew it all along."

Two weeks later, she had a stroke and became a compliant body with a Raggedy Ann doll across her bosom and tubes running in and out of her. I was relieved that I couldn't see what raged there.

Vida was busy and I felt flabby. I holed up for a week. What came out was a field-stripped deer hanging from a limb, a bull covering a cow and a catfish nailed to a cottonwood for skinning.

I felt good. I'd made up my mind to marry Vida and take her away. Which wasn't going to be easy.

Her desktop publishing was booming with treatises and handbooks: what to eat, How to make love, How to bathe the baby, cooperation not competition, evolution not revolution, love not hate, how to fight fires, how to form a bank, goodbye greed, on being disputatious, the illusions of freedom, the good and evil of freedom, the threads of chaos and fate, Augustine was wrong, how to douche properly, destruction and creation, how to do the colonic, how to cut the umbilical cord, how to bury the dead, how to look at a picture, how to read a poem, how to make good whiskey, how to deal with the outside, goodbye original sin, worms and viruses, trojan horses, how to be commercial and survive, the joys of confusion and cataclysms, communities and faces, how to fix a car, interchange and contentment.

Despite the outpouring, all wasn't smooth at the school. The impatient Hillman Doe was more and more of a presence calling for fast not slow. The world was teeming. It was time to tear off a new country, to rip the fabric and reweave it. All that was needed was a big bang.

The stories about the school raking in gobs of money from a marijuana plantation in the woods didn't die. Four bodies, one FBI, one CIA, one Colombian, one local paramilitary, were found with their throats slit ear to ear.

Things got tighter than a gnat's ass. Hillman Doe lit out for the Mexican hills, leaving Esperanza behind. She didn't smile when I told her she'd be better off. She thanked me and said quietly it was none of my business.

FBI, CIA, Texas Rangers, local law, media, and whoever stomped around eager to jail anyone who so much as looked crossways at them, which meant Vida in particular.

When the marijuana processor was found, the media screamed that it was time to attack. Our security demanded it. The forces of law and order and good had stood still long enough.

Tarred with all sorts of brushes, Vida smiled and kept on with what she was doing.

Next to Vida, Ronnie was the sanest. He did his dead-level best to curb the intruding authorities, his deputies and the citizenry. I hate to admit it, but Old Joe of the bloody nose did yeoman work. He and Vida and a couple of groups who disagreed about everything but a belief in civil liberty did their best to dam the newly unchained purity.

I was left on the outskirts. The fight was hard and all consuming for Vida.

I welded a few sturdy benches with life-like figures on them for the school. I did a sculpture of a boar ready for coupling or fighting.

I loved Vida but I had mixed feelings about the school. Vida had asked me more than once to teach at the school, but I said no. I wasn't one of those who said if one can, one does, and if one cannot, one teaches. —Vida proved teaching was doing. —I was afraid the teaching would dominate, that I would no longer be the itinerant painter I was.

I couldn't get to Vida to ask her to marry me. So I waited and hoped Vida would find time for my itchy feet and the nomad in me.

2

Just to hear someone say, "See you, got to be movin' on" or "Got places to go and things to see" or "I'll be moseying along" or "Time to hit the road" sent shivers through me.

I tried to tell Dorothy how I felt, but she was too busy to do more than to say hello.

I told my mother, but she wasn't in this world and wherever she was, she was likely to be there after I was long gone.

Nothing to do but barge in on Vida.

She was making faces at herself in the mirror. "I'm practicing my death mask," she said with an unabashed grin.

"That sounds like fun," I shucked my clothes without another word.

She shucked hers and we lay and hugged and kissed and talked. She was all aglow.

The time was ripe to ask her but I didn't. I feared I'd make a fool of myself. I don't know why that bothered me, it never had. But what if I asked Vida and she laughed and said,

"No, Good Lord, no! How could you imagine the two of us, you and me, married to each other? Wayman, you silly old man."

What if she said Yes? Would she nail my feet to the floor of her school?

I shivered. I loved her; yes, I did. I know I did. But once she'd irritated me to the point where I'd painted her face in a mare's pussy. A picture I kept hidden.

But I loved her and wanted to make her my seventh. She was my natural.

So, I lay there watching, afraid to say a word.

Without warning she said, "I've missed you. I have something to tell you."

I froze.

"Betty and I did bury a few fetuses in the yard. I suppose you think that was wrong of us."

"You had your reasons."

"You ever think of your funeral, Wayman?"

"I believe we've had this conversation before."

"Sorry," she said and caressed my chest, then laid her head on my bosom.

"When I was a very young man, I used to imagine lots of big-titted women trying to raise my temporal body from the grave. Lots of mourners and lots of music."

"I used to compose. I could dash off a tone poem."

"I quit that fantasy years ago."

"Even the big tits?"

"Even the big tits."

She looked coy and said, "My tits used to be bigger."

"Your breasts are fine," I said, ready to ask her, but she cut me off.

"Isn't it interesting? You said, 'my temporal body' as if you had a non-temporal body."

"Beg pardon." She had thrown me another of her unexpected curves.

"Our language traps us and our senses deceive. We say *temporal body* in the hope we'll have another after this one wears out."

"It's just a manner of speaking," I said, annoyed we were off on one of her intellectual adventures. "Besides people have to have hope," I said remembering Carla.

"Nonsense. People live every day of their lives without hope. People are stronger than you think. We need many things to survive, but contrary to the popular notion, we don't need hope. Believe me, I know."

I didn't know what to say, so we lay there and held each other until I said, "Well, hope or no hope, you do love life."

"I'm not so sure. Sometimes I think it's more curiosity than love. But I have felt the flow of love. I've never trusted those who love life with capital L's."

Oh, God? How could I tell her I loved her and wanted to marry her? There was no hope for it, no fucking hope at all.

She raised herself on her right elbow and looked me over as if she was going to wash me away with her words.

"I feel that surge now," she said and walked her fingers across my chest. "I think we should get married. You'd be my first husband. So, what'd you think? Will you marry me?"

"Yes," I felt like I'd fallen off a cliff.

"I want to get married then be gone from here. I don't want to be buried where I was born. You agree?"

"Oh yes." The fall from the cliff didn't kill me. It made me bounce.

3

Getting married was more than having a ceremony. I packed and repacked and culled. I decided to take only the paintings I figured would sell.

I gave the place a good cleaning, to the point of chasing snakes out of the well. I liked my house and the comfort it gave. Lorrain and the boy would look after it. Esperanza might take a lover in it. The house encouraged love.

So did the open road. I wasn't sad to leave.

I finished and went to help Vida. I'd never seen her in such a rage.

"Don't fuck with me," she said. "My blood's up."

I tried to look as calm and as peaceful as possible. I was afraid she'd changed her mind.

"You know how it is when you're killing snakes. You get caught up in the hacking. You warm to the act. The hackles on your neck grow as erect as any penis ever was. You swirl in the killing. Your blood makes dogs howl. Everything about you is geared for the doing. You rise to the thrill. Motion is all. There is no time to ponder. There is no time for skepticism. There is nothing to distract you. There is only the beauty of swinging a pickaxe."

"What's happened?"

She wiped her face. "Nothing, except that's the way I feel when I clean house, so don't fuck with me."

"How about a glass of water?"

"Fine." She plopped down on the davenport and waved at dust floating in the light. She took a sip.

"You better think twice before hooking up with me. I'm not always easy."

"Don't I know it," I said. I wondered if she'd changed her mind.

She sipped and said, "A judge once told me I was a crime against nature, a woman who wanted to grow a penis. I asked that misguided student of the law why in the world would I want a penis when I have a vagina and a clitoris that won't quit." She grinned. "He didn't know what a clitoris was." She finished the water.

"I was a long tall drink of water who whipped up the wind. Men liked to bump up against me and say 'All you need is a good . . . '"

"Thrashing?" I teased.

"Fucking." She laughed. "What Vida Singer needed was frequent fucking. —Good and forceful and frequent. Fucking was what I needed, all right." She licked her lips.

"How silly! I could outscrew any ten of them. —Does that make you jealous?"

"No," I said, which wasn't completely true.

"Still want to marry these damaged goods?"

"Yes."

"Then give me an hour and I'll be ready."

4

True to her word she was ready in an hour. She was resplendent in her royal purple dress and high heels. One of her classic hats added to her wonder.

Ronnie ramrodded the license, gathered the crowd, arranged for the organist, strung a banner "GOODBYE AND GOD BLESS" and performed the ceremony.

With Jake gone and the Busters in decline, Ronnie was top dog in Sage County.

The ceremony was plain and sweet. "I, Wayman, I, Vida, take you for better or worse." And we kissed.

Dorothy sang "Amazing Grace," which I thought was strange for a wedding. Esperanza and Lorrain cried. The boy kept wiping his eyes. Old Joe kept a respectable distance. None of my exes or kids showed. My mother sat in a wheelchair in the shade.

Ronnie got carried away when he kissed Vida and said, "God bless you and keep you."

The giddy Vida said, "We'll need all the help we can get."

Her students tried to give us the world, but we didn't have room for it in the truck.

Finally the party was over. We climbed into the truck, man and wife, female and husband, and headed west.

5

The sun was high, the sky clear and deep and blue. Everything was crisp and clean, sharp and detailed, with no haze or smog.

Vida stuck a pillow behind her head and rested against the door. Her face relaxed, she smiled and closed her eyes. The lines showed more clearly, but they weren't the lines of death. I reached to touch her hand. She sighed and a smile crossed her lips.

"Wanderlust," she murmured. "When I was young, I was full of storm and stress. I whipped up the wind. I wanted to embrace the world, to save it from itself. I wanted to spread the truth and free the oppressed—and the oppressors.

"I tumpted over icons and people tumpted back." She grinned. "I had expected their gratitude, but what I got was 'Go away, you bother me'. I didn't, not as they say, of my own volition."

"I can believe that," I said.

"They didn't understand that I was the new Joan of Arc. Smoke came out of their nostrils. They wanted to burn me at the stake, but I kept pissing it out. Which reminds me."

We stopped. She got out and made water on a surprised sidewinder.

"There's nothing like a good pee." She got back in. "Where was I? . . . Religious and economic dogma are tough things to attack. Galileo was pretty slick."

I'd always taken my non-religion, if that's the correct term, as a matter of course. My economic creed, if any, was to survive without stomping on others.

"So," she said, "I went from place to place. I was among the youngest to protest World War One. I didn't protest World War Two.

"I had trouble making a living, so I went to Hollywood with a body that wouldn't quit. I didn't change the world, but I made some very funny blue comedies, one involving a goat. I didn't make love to the goat. I tricked the male lead into thinking the goat was me. —And one art film in which I dressed up like a man in love with a woman who loved a burro. Very avant-garde.

"My co-star fell in love with that burro. She claimed he was very attentive."

She brushed her dress, gave me a quiet giggle and looked at me with mischievous and seductive eyes.

"Enormous penises alone have never held much interest for me, except as something to see." More tease, more giggles. "I must say, once one did leave me comfortably sore, if not mentally fulfilled. —Does that make you jealous?"

It did, but I wouldn't let her know. I smiled and said, "No."

"Anyway, I never mated with animal or beast until you came along."

"Thank you."

"What am I saying? Why am I telling you these things? —Oh, well, never mind, Miss Betty saved me."

She went quiet for a few miles, looking out the window at the spaces, then said,

"A life by itself is lonely enough. Miss Betty and I didn't mind being on the outside, but most people have trouble with isolation. They want to belong. So we set out to develop a plan whereby individuals could find a niche in this old world. Not so easy."

"I can see that," I said. I was timid when it came to her ideas. I smiled and sucked up my guts and said, "Until now, I've been a roadrunner all my life. I walk along with someone or some thing then I move on. I'm a born roamer —not a drifter, but a roamer—an itinerant artist, a peddler. I've never seen myself any other way. I don't see much room for peddler artists in your community."

She smiled to show me she wasn't angry. "You may be right. We're both itinerants. It would be a shame to lose that. Even so, we belong to each other. We have a lot to learn, even now."

Before I could answer, we were hit by a rainstorm from out of nowhere so thick it was like driving in a river. We were no sooner out of that than we ran into a quick hailstorm. Then we hit a stretch were it was raining in a straight line on the right, while on the left tumbleweeds hurtled by with the sun shining in the distance.

"A lot of wise people say human nature is fixed. I don't believe it. We haven't gotten anywhere near the boundaries yet." She leaned over and gave me a peck on the cheek. "I don't know. It all looks so haphazard. Like something essential's been lost."

"Maybe that's why some people look to the Divine." I almost didn't say that.

She came alive. "Wayman, you surprise me. Do you think the Divine's the answer?"

"No, not really, yes, well, I don't know. I'm comfortable with my non-religion. I suppose some folks would say it remains to be seen." I smiled. I felt more comfortable talking about former lovers. "What about Hillman Doe? You all ever . . . ?"

"Not that I can recall," she laughed. "Hillman's a man in a hurry. He thinks if you grab people by their pussies, their hearts and minds are sure to follow. He sees a new country now."

"A man to be watched."

"I like him, but I watch him."

She looked across the country. "I love badlands. A body can get lost and still do so much."

I thought, So much for belonging, but didn't say a word. I looked toward the horizon. The plateau on the left looked like a woman ready to take her lover with her breasts pointing up, her belly soft and curved, joined at her mound by long supple legs. Next to her a man lay stretched out on his side, his penis firm, ready to mount. I felt a quiver. Vida and I had not yet solemnized the occasion in our fashion.

"I'm hungry," she said. We stopped at a small cafe. I hustled some sketches for our meals. It was good to be on the road. It was like old times. I felt like I was doing what I was cut out for, what I was best at.

I said, "What I need is a good mall."

She said, "What we need is a place to sleep."

We found this small, clean motel in the middle of the desert. The night was clear and the stars were out.

Vida said, "Time to consummate."

We made love with more vigor than usual. It felt good when she stuck her tongue in my mouth. I have no other words to describe our lovemaking, except to say I'd never been so happy.

6

The next morning I did a pretty good watercolor of the sunrise, then went out and got some fruit for breakfast. When I got back, Vida was sitting upright in bed. I offered her a banana, which she peeled slowly.

"I was just remembering," she said as she ate, "how some of my judges prophesied that if I didn't confess and repent, I'd wind up eating grass and growing hair down to my ankles, that my nails would grow as long as an eagle's claws. —I thought, The better to scratch your eyes out. —Some said I was going to go crazy like a female Nebuchadnezzar. I fooled them."

She looked like a proud child, then said, "I think we ought to get ourselves a portable TV station."

"A what?"

"A TV station. A floating one, like a ship at sea."

"There're no oceans around here," I said as softly as I could.

"True. Only miles and miles of the loveliest badlands you ever saw. We have a fax, a computer, and wireless phones. All we need is some equipment and an eighteen-wheeler with an antenna. We'd have a moveable feast."

"Somehow I don't see myself wrestling an eighteen-wheeler all over the place."

"I know you don't, but I do."

"I don't know a thing about TV stations," I said.

"Not to worry. We have the money and the mental resources. I'd make a hell of a pundit. So would you."

"I don't know."

"Nothing to know. It's easy."

"I want to do what I do best, is all," I said.

"I won't keep you from your work." She gave me her most persuasive look. "You game, Wayman?"

My first thought was, I'm too old for this shit. The second was a hundred-eighty-degree turn; there's nothing wrong in taking on something new. Keeps you alive, young, crazy, whatever.

"I'm game," I said.

"Wayman, we're going to have one fine Fucking Grade A life. We fucking-A will. Yes!"

"Vida, are you all right?"

"I apologize. I shouldn't use the language so much. When I was young, I hoarded the words. Nowadays, they pour out."

"No matter," I said.

"Oh, it matters all right," she said. "You sure you're okay?"

"Fine as frog's hair. You?"

"Fine as frog's hair." I felt more than lucky to love her and have her love me.

We finished eating, cleaned up, loaded the truck and scooted. I felt like I did when I was a boy and got my first taste of pure wildness.

"All my life, what I've hated almost more than anything is for someone to tell me to act my age," Vida said and looked at me with a walleyed smile. "Hardly married and already I like it." She closed her eyes and slept the better part of three hours.

I drove steadily, wanting to stop several times. There was so much to paint.

She sighed and stretched. She looked warm and good.

"Oh, me. I didn't mean to sleep so long." She stretched better than a cat.

"I don't mean to go all gushy, but the thing is, look joyfully on the coming day. You agree?"

"No matter what it brings?"

"No matter what it brings. You know, Wayman, I have the oddest feeling that if I should die now, I'd be fulfilled. Of course, I'm not going to die now. I have too much to do. I don't mean to sound like Pollyanna. But the joy of life is not a trick. I learned that the hard way." She took a deep breath and watched my reaction.

She laughed, "I don't mean capital JOY OF LIFE. Screw that. I mean something different, something not so easy."

I thought, What can I lose by pitching tents with a woman who has no fear of living beyond the pale? I'll be all right, at least most of the time.